Don't Tell Mom I Have a Girlfriend

DON'T TELL MOM I HAVE A GIRLFRIEND

Hatfield Falls (Don't Tell) Book 1

ANNILEE NELSON

LEENIE B BOOKS
HALIFAX

ABOUT HATFIELD FALLS

Welcome to Hatfield Falls, an imaginary town set in the beautiful province of Nova Scotia, Canada. This series focuses on several individuals in that town who are related by blood and/or their connections at Hatfield Falls Christian Church.

Faith, hope, and love flow here in great streams and small trickles. However, these streams don't take happy easy paths. Instead, they swerve around obstacles, dredge up memories from the past, cascade over plans for the present, and push the characters of Hatfield Falls forward into a future that is firmly rooted in grace and grounded in Christ.

CHAPTER 1

"It is a truth universally acknowledged –"

"Mother! It's a cookie." Will Bennett rubbed the sore spot between his eyes. His mother often made that part of his head hurt when she got into one of her moods, such as she was in today. "Even Edmund would tell you that the line you are quoting is an excellent example of sarcasm. Therefore, if you say that it is a truth universally acknowledged that a man with a cup of tea is in want of a cookie, doesn't that mean that a man in possession of a cup of tea is actually *NOT* looking for a cookie at all?"

He looked for support from his younger brother, Edmund, who nodded his agreement – not that their mother saw him do it. A verbal response would have been more effective.

"Fitzwilliam." His mother used her scolding-a-toddler voice and wiggled the plate she held in front of him.

1

Will closed his eyes and sighed as he shook his head. Why did she take such pleasure in tormenting him? Wasn't the eldest son supposed to be the most beloved?

"My name is not Fitzwilliam, Mother. It's William. Just William. No Fitz."

His mother, Amy Bennett, a diminutive woman whose size belied her ability to be moved on a point if she did not wish to be moved, rolled her eyes and shot a displeased look at his father. "That's only because your father wouldn't allow it."

"Yes, I know, and that's why he's my favourite parent."

"Your father couldn't bake a proper oatmeal cookie if he tried," she scoffed as she placed one on the edge of Will's saucer.

Sunday afternoon teatime at the Bennet home couldn't be had with mere mugs. No, his mother insisted upon cups that were made for the beverage. Mugs were for cocoa and coffee and pretty much anything else anyone wanted to drink from them, but they were not proper beverage containers when it was time for tea. On Sundays, in Mrs. Bennett's living room, only fine porcelain cups and saucers were allowed.

He sighed. Whether he wished to have a cookie or

not, he was having one – or – Will eyed Thor – feeding it to the dog when his mother wasn't looking.

"Father makes them with chocolate chunks, you know – not raisins – which, by the way, is the second reason he's my favourite parent," he called after his mother as she moved on to torment her next child.

"I don't mind being your second favorite parent," she said with a teasing grin.

She rarely seemed phased by his foul moods or taunting words. Will could grumble up a hurricane and still she would, most often, respond with a smile. She was a patient, though annoying, parent.

"Do not feed that cookie to Mr. Thorpe," she added.

"His name is Thor, Mother, not Mr. Thorpe."

"You may call him what you want, but he is Mr. Thorpe to me and is not to have any cookies."

"Then, why did you give me one?" Will asked bluntly. The dull throbbing in his head was not getting any better. Laughter might be deemed a good medicine for the soul, but levity did not work as well as peace and quiet, augmented by a proper dose of analgesic, when it came to headaches.

"Here," Emma handed him a bottle of pain medicine. "I'll trade you two of these for one cookie."

"I thought you weren't eating carbs?"

"Do you want the medicine or not?" Emma hissed

as she darted a look at their mother. "It's Sunday, and I'm allowing myself as many carbs as I want today."

Will pulled his head back a bit and quickly handed her his cookie with one hand, while snatching the medicine bottle from her with the other. "You may want to eat more carbs all the other days of the week, too," he suggested.

She scowled at him.

"Sorry," he muttered. He disliked it when Emma was angry with him, and normally, she was quite receptive to his grumbling and unsolicited advice. "Are you okay?"

"Don't ask," she replied. "At least, not right now."

His brow furrowed.

"Mother," she mouthed.

Ah, yes. There were things you did not say in front of the Bennett matriarch. Of course, Will could not think of what Emma might need to keep quiet that was making her pop cookies into her mouth like they were popcorn and she was watching a rom-com.

"Outside?" he asked.

She nodded. "But don't make it obvious, Will. Please, try to be subtle."

"I'll try," he assured her. He drained the last bit of tea from his cup so he could swallow the medicine Emma had given him and stood.

"And where do you think you're going?" his

mother asked. There was a hint of displeasure to her tone. Apparently, she was coming close to the edge of her ability to be long-suffering.

He lifted his cup. "Water."

"You haven't told me about your week."

He stood where he was and began a list of the highlights of his life – the bits he knew she wanted to know. "All the paperwork about the land has been transferred. My new office is on-site. The development plans are being drawn up, and my bank account is still in the black." Although success was still an ever-present worry, but what was new about that?

"I have had no dates." Not that he would tell her if he had. "Nor have I met anyone who inspires me to go on a date." Again, not that he would tell her if he had. Some things were better kept to oneself until they were certain and set. He'd made that mistake once, and he wasn't the sort to repeat horrible disasters if it could be avoided.

"And, I won't name my land development project *Pemberley Shores* just because my name is William Bennett, and the name seems fitting." He held up a hand to prevent the protest he knew his mother was going to give. "Not even if it could bring sales from people like you."

"He wants sane tenants," Henry quipped.

"Boys." Mark Bennett's tone was stern – the sort of

stern that drew Will and his brothers up short, even now when they were all well into their adult years. Just because he was thirty didn't mean that Will did not still have a healthy respect for the things, like his father's tone just now, that told him that he had gone too far.

"I didn't say it," Will protested.

"But you were thinking it," his father retorted.

That was true, he had been thinking it. He just was not as prone to say what he was thinking as Henry was, for Henry was a terrific tease.

Whether Will had said it or not, he knew he owed his mother an apology of sorts, so he blew out a breath, crossed the living room to where his mother was sitting, kissed her cheek, and said, "Thank you for the dinner and tea, Mother. I am going to get some water, and then, I'll see if," he grimaced, "Mr. Thorpe would like to take a quick turn of the back garden." That sounded period drama enough to soothe his mother's ruffled feathers. At least, he hoped it did, for, despite her annoying habit of tormenting him about getting married, he loved her dearly. "I'll be back soon."

And with that, he made a hasty retreat from the living room, through the dining room, and into the kitchen before anything further could be said.

~*~

The screen door squeaked as William pushed his way out to the back steps with a glass of water in one hand and Thor at his heels.

The happy mutt bounded down the steps and raced to the back fence where he sniffed along the bottom of it before making a wandering path back towards the house. His nose never left the ground until he found just the perfect spot to do what he needed to do. Then, he kicked up the grass and raced off to inspect the far corner of the fence on the side of the yard that was connected by a gate to the neighbour's yard.

Will leaned against the deck's railing and watched Thor amuse himself while waiting for Emma.

How many times had William raced off to that gate himself over the years? He and Nate were always at each other's homes back before university and adulthood had separated them somewhat. Be that as it may, they were still quite often together; but then, that's what happens when one friend goes into business with another.

"Oh, aren't you looking happy today?" Mrs. Clark, Nate's mom, reached over the fence to scratch Thor's ear. Then, she waved at Will. "Are you all home today?"

Will pushed off from the railing against which he was leaning and walked towards the gate. "No, Brandon is still away, but the rest of us are all in there." He nodded toward the house.

"I suppose I would have known that if I had made it to church today," she apologized.

"I suppose you would have, but we aren't keeping score. And you have a very good reason to not have been at church."

She smiled. It was an expression he cherished. Mrs. Clark was like a second mother to him, but without the drive to tease him like his own mother possessed. Her smile was also an expression he had feared he might never see again after her diagnosis six months ago.

"I do like that about your parents, Will. Unlike some pastoral couples I knew when I was growing up, your parents are quite normal."

Will chuckled. "I'm not sure my mother has ever been normal."

"Oh, go on with you," Mrs. Clark said as she swatted the air in his direction and laughed. "I find your mother to be delightful."

"That's only because you like the same things she does," Will retorted. "But just try being her son who has no interest in period dramas or romance novels."

"Jane Austen did not write romance novels. She wrote classics."

To Will, any book that centered on a guy and girl

getting married was a romance novel. However, it was not a point he wished to argue about today. Instead, he decided to focus on the second half of Mrs. Clark's defense. "Do you suppose Miss Austen thought her stories would be classics when she wrote them?"

"I would hope that any author who summons up enough courage to put pen to paper and then see their creation enjoyed by others would expect their work to become a classic one day."

She had responded as he had hoped she would.

"Even if it's a classic romance novel?" he asked with a grin.

Her lips pursed and her eyes sparkled. She had always been more pleasant to tease about these things than his mother ever was. Mother took things far too seriously – especially when it came to Jane Austen.

"Even if it is a classic romance *short story*," she agreed.

Will could not help but chuckle at that. "Don't let Edmund hear you say that. He thinks all genre fiction is drivel and anything that takes less than forever to read is a waste of time and paper."

"He does know that most books are now published without the need for paper, doesn't he?" Her tone was laughing. They both knew that Edmund had some very traditional opinions about what was and what was not worthy of a person's reading time.

"He rues the day that the e-book was invented."

"Yet, he praises the ability to stream a six-hour miniseries."

"That is the conundrum that is Edmund Bennett." Will's younger-by-six-years brother had only recently graduated with a degree in English and was currently finishing up a certificate program through the local library's employment initiative. Not only did Eddie have a degree he liked to flaunt as proof that his opinions were correct, but he now also had a job where he could share those opinions with fellow snobbish bookworms like himself.

"Oh, isn't Emma looking more like your mom every day?" This outburst, accompanied by the squeak of the back door, let Will know that his sister had finally sneaked out of the living room and was waiting for him.

"She does look a lot like Mother." And a lot less like the kid sister he had known for nearly twenty years. He wasn't certain he was ready for her to be grown up. However, she had been out of high school for a full year, and it was likely time he began to make peace with that.

Emma skipped down the steps and waved as she crossed the yard. "Mrs. Clark! Are you feeling better?"

"I'm well enough to talk to a neighbor and clean my

own dishes, but I'm not well enough to go out in public and have to be pleasant," she replied with a laugh.

"I'm happy to hear it," Emma replied. "What did the doctor say when you last saw him?"

"He thinks the treatments have done their duty, so that is behind me. Now, I must work on recovery from the treatments and continue a course of some medications."

Emma held her hand out to Mrs. Clark. "That's excellent news! I've been praying for you."

"And baking me casseroles and cookies." Mrs. Clark squeezed Emma's hand. "You are such a dear to see to my sweet tooth and tempt my appetite with your cooking. Even chemo couldn't keep me from a little taste of your food now and then."

"Do you still have enough in the freezer?"

Emma was the very embodiment of compassion and hospitality. In that way, she was also like their mother. Only, in Emma, the trait seemed effortless. For their mother, it was not always quite as easy. But then again, Emma was nineteen, and she did not have a husband and six children.

William caught himself before he visibly shuddered at the idea of his baby sister as a wife and mother. He needed to get used to the idea of her being an adult before he even started trying to accept that she was now old enough to marry.

Mrs. Clark did visibly shudder – or rather, she shivered – and rubbed her arms. "I do hope that once my body starts to recover, I'll be able to enjoy an early Nova Scotia summer day without a sweater and for longer than a few minutes." She tipped her face towards the sun. "I cannot tell you how good it is to feel the sun on my face – without a window between it and me. God is good."

She reached over the gate and scratched Thor's ear again. "Nathaniel said that your business plans are going well, Will."

"They are. I hope to have a model home or two ready before school begins in September."

She nodded. "He told me that it wouldn't be long until you had some homes up and ready to tour, but, being his mother and knowing how enthusiastic my son can be about projects when they first begin, I wasn't sure if his timetable was accurate or not."

"Oh, I'm certain we won't have the model home ready quickly enough for Nate," Will replied with a laugh.

Nathaniel Clark was exuberance and energy personified. However, he was also the best contractor Will had ever done business with. Nate cared deeply about getting things right, not just getting them done, but that did not mean he worked slowly. No, Nate knew how to push his crew to meet some pretty spectacularly quick deadlines without alienating any of them.

"I'm sure you are correct about that," Mrs. Clark said, "and I will tell you what I told him: I want to be one of the first to tour your first home. I should be doing quite well by the time one is ready."

"I'd be honoured to have you at our first, invitation-only, open house, which is on my calendar in pencil for the third weekend in August. How does that sound?"

"Perfect. I wouldn't miss it for the world. I'm proud of you boys." She held up a hand to keep Will from speaking. "I've faced my mortality, Will Bennett, and I will tell those I love how much I love them whenever I want to do so. None of us know how many more times we will have to do things like that, but I know that fact better than most. You and Nate are doing something special. It takes guts to start a business, especially one that is a bit on the unusual side of things."

She turned as if she was going to return to her house, but then turned back. "And I will tell you that your mother is also quite proud of her enterprising son. I know she is not the sort to say things like that to you very often, but I have heard the pride in her voice when she speaks about you and your plans." She smiled. "Are you certain you wouldn't consider her suggestion for the name?"

"*Pemberley Shores?*" Will asked in surprise.

Mrs. Clark nodded. "There are some who would buy a home at over market value if it had the name Pemberley attached to it." She chuckled.

Will shook his head. He wasn't actually creating this development that he had planned for larger-than-life returns.

"It was worth a try. Give my best to your parents, and Emma, I have not forgotten about you. I would love for you to come for a visit and tell me about your plans for next year. And at some point, I would like to see your new accommodations."

"I would love to show them to you," Emma said. "And I promise to stop by one day next week."

With a wave, Mrs. Clark left them to return to her house.

"What has Mother done to cause you stress?" Will glanced nervously at the house. He knew that they'd been gone for a while and soon, someone would come in search of them, ending any chance they had to talk privately. Alone time was not something to be found in great quantities in a large, tightly-knit family like his.

"She's done nothing except to be her normal self."

Will's brow furrowed. "Then, what's the issue?"

"I am not going to Bible college. I never applied, and I've not told Mom or Dad about it, and Mom has started talking about getting what I need to take with me when I leave."

Well, that was surprising. Emma had always done what her parents wanted her to do without protest, even when she didn't really want to do it. "What will you do instead?" He knew she had to have a plan, for just like him, she always seemed to have a plan.

"I've signed up to take a few culinary courses at the community college."

"Culinary courses you say?" That seemed a good fit for his kitchen-loving sister.

She nodded. "I want to open a café."

"You do? That sounds like a good idea." He could see her doing well as a café owner – once she had completed her studies, which he hoped included business courses.

"I do, and I think I may have found a business partner."

Will blinked. "You have?" That seemed sudden.

"I met her at one of the cooking classes I attended in March. She was actually the guest presenter."

"Have you only met her once?" Choosing a business partner was no small thing. One must know the person well enough to trust them and know that your values matched. In his opinion, one meeting was not enough for that.

Emma shook her head. "No, I've gone to two singles' nights with her at her church in Marydale, which I know is a drive from here, but she is moving to Hatfield Falls in August."

"Three meetings and you think she's trustworthy enough to be your business partner?" Will wouldn't say it outright to his baby sister, but, at present, he was thinking she was nuts.

"I know. I know. It is crazy, but Will, she's perfect. We get along so well. It's as if we have been friends for years and not just a few months. We talk online, too. I am not just basing my evaluation on three meetings." She broke eye contact with him, turning her head to look at something to their right. "I would like you to meet her before I tell Mom about my plans."

He could do that, he supposed. "Do the two of you have a business plan drawn up?"

Emma shook her head. "We are only in the beginning phases of planning, and Cari is still looking for a place in Hatfield Falls. I thought..."

"That I might know of a place she could afford?"

"Yes. Housing isn't cheap here, which is why you're creating your estate as you are." Her eyes had found his again. "Will you, please, meet with us tomorrow?"

"Tomorrow?"

"Around nine in the morning? Nate said he didn't see anything on your schedule."

Will's eyes grew wide at that. His friend knew about his sister's plans before he did? That didn't seem right!

"He doesn't know why I wanted to know if you were free, Will. Relax. You are still my favourite eldest brother."

"I'm your only *eldest* brother. Can't you just admit that I am your favourite older brother?"

"No," she said with a shake of her head. "You guys get way too competitive at trying to prove you're the best at things."

"Not all of us. It's mostly just Henry and Fred."

She snorted in disbelief. "Right. And if I said Edmund was my favourite older brother, what would you do?"

Will shrugged. "I'd let him meet this stranger you have befriended, and then, go tell Mother you aren't going to go to Bible college to find a husband."

The comment was met by the laughter he knew it deserved.

"Exactly. It is all of you, and not just Henry and Fred, although I will admit that they are the worst for it."

"Mom is starting to think Will left because she tried to make him eat raisins," Henry called from the back door. There was the sound of something being shouted inside the house, and then, Henry laughed.

"Why does she let him do things for her? She

should know by now that he is going to do his best to torment her in the process."

"Because," Emma said as she wrapped her arm around Will's, "he's always the first to want to know what is going on. They are a lot alike, aren't they?"

"Indubitably," he agreed as they started walking toward the house. "So, nine tomorrow morning?"

"Yes."

"Where?"

She nodded toward what used to be the family's garage that stood across the alley from their fenced yard. "My place."

CHAPTER 2

"I thought you were going to teach a class at the grocery store." Lacey Welsh felt irritation welling inside her. Her sister, Cari, had not bothered to tell her that this was a longer-than-normal trip to Hatfield Falls today.

"I am. I'm just stopping at Emma's house first to meet her brother."

"About a business plan?" Lacey knew that this whole idea of starting a café was not a new one for Cari, but it was new that she was considering starting a café *now* and in a new town.

"Yep. Emma and I would like to have things sorted before classes begin in the fall."

"Classes and starting a café? In the same year?"

Cari grinned. "In the same month, actually."

"Are you actually crazy or just playing at it today?" Blood pressure medication was in Lacey's near future. She could feel it. Ever since last year, when Cari had been dumped by her long-time boyfriend, things with her had changed from doing the expected to pushing the bounds of acceptability.

First, it had been a drastic haircut – from mid-back to just below her ears – and colour – from her lovely natural chestnut to a deep red and then a purple and now pink. As if those changes had not been shocking enough, there had also been leaving school after only one year of general business admin classes to become a cooking class presenter for a chain of stores.

Now, it seemed, that even the shifting and less than steady work of teaching classes was about to be replaced by the even less stable proposition of starting a business with a girl who was three years younger than her and had even less experience.

Cari had turned in her seat, so she was facing Lacey. "No, Lacey, I'm neither crazy, nor am I pretending to be. This is me – or at least, I think it's me. I never wanted to be an office administrator or branch manager or any other such title. I only thought I did because it would make Braydon happy. I'm done making anyone else happy, Lacey. It's time I do what I want to do. I have always loved cooking, and you have to admit that I'm good at it."

Lacey could not deny that. Cari's cooking had been the best part of her moving back in with Lacey after their mother died.

"But school and a new business? At the same time?" Couldn't her sister see how that was not a good combination?

"Why do I need to wait?"

"Because both are going to require a lot of time and energy." Not to mention money.

"I'm taking one class, Lacey. One. I think I'll have time to manage a café during the rest of my time."

"And who will manage the café when you are in class? From what you told me earlier, Emma is also going to take classes."

"She's only taking enough to keep her mother happy."

Lacey shook her head. "Do you hear yourself?"

"What's wrong with what I said? Emma's mother wants her to go to college – Bible college – to find a husband."

Lacey, who could hear her sister's eyes rolling as she said the word husband, shot Cari a skeptical look. Surely, no one's mother sent their daughter to school just to get a husband.

"And get a degree," Cari added.

Ah, that's what Lacey thought. Emma's mom probably just hoped her daughter would find a nice guy to date in the process of getting a degree. Again, she could not fault a mother for wanting that for her daughter. "Getting a degree is not a bad thing."

"It is if it's *not* the degree for something that you *know* you're supposed to be doing." Cari turned away from her and folded her arms like a shield across her chest.

Lacey blew out a calming breath. She hated disagreements, and honestly, Lacey was not attempting to start the argument about Cari's future without a college education again. She had made her peace – mostly – with the fact that her little sister was taking a new and rather unconventional path.

"Ok, explain. I know you haven't been exactly happy for over a year now. How do you know that this exciting venture is what you are supposed to be doing and not just a fun diversion from everything that has happened?" She held up two fingers to let her sister know this was going to be a two-part question. "And... how does Emma know?"

Lacey liked Emma. She seemed like a good, well-grounded young woman. Or she had until this morning, when Cari had shared their plan to start a business as soon as was humanly possible, if not sooner.

"Do you remember three months ago at the ladies' retreat when the speaker talked about leaving your mark on the next generation?" Cari asked.

Lacey nodded. She had been quite affected by that message and doubted she would ever forget it.

"I started praying about what God wanted me to do. I told Him all about my desires and asked if He would show me if He was in them or if I needed to find new ones."

That seemed like a good and, dare she say it, responsible thing to do.

"The next month, I met Emma, and we clicked. The next month after, she told me about her dilemma with her mom wanting her to go to college and her not wanting to go to that college and all that." Cari was once again turned in Lacey's direction. Excitement oozed from her pores. "She told me – *before* I told her anything about what I had been praying about – that she had been praying for God to confirm for her the decision she had made about her future before she presented it to her parents."

"And she wanted to start a café?"

"No! Well, yes, but not yet. She wanted to take culinary classes and then start a café."

"So, you're saying Emma wants to wait, but you are forging ahead with your plan anyway?"

Cari huffed. "You sure know how to suck the joy out of everything, don't you?"

"I'm not trying to be a joy-sucker. I am trying to help you avoid disaster." She was doing her job as the older sister.

"My prayer had been for God to provide a dream

23

sharer – someone who wanted the same thing as I did, who had a love for Him and was unafraid to move in an unconventional way. Emma is all of those things, Lacey. Don't you see? Emma is God's answer to my prayer. She has always wanted to cook and have a café. She not only loves the Lord, but her father is the pastor of the church I will be attending when I move here, and have you seen the news reports about the new housing development going in in Hatfield Falls?"

"The one with houses made out of shipping containers?" She had heard about that and thought it sounded like an interesting idea.

Cari nodded. "That's Emma's brother's project. She has told me all about it and is always so excited by the idea that I think that qualifies Emma as someone who is not afraid of the unconventional."

Lacey had to admit that her sister was not moving ahead without due consideration. However, that still did not make it an easy plan for Lacey to willingly endorse. "You're certain about this? It won't be easy."

"Lacey, I've tried easy – I picked the hot guy with the promising future, I made sure I was all that a guy like that would want as his wife when he strikes it rich, and what has that gotten me? Nothing more than a broken heart."

Lacey reached over and squeezed Cari's knee. Her sister's heart had been more than broken. It had been shattered, which was the only reason Lacey could find for her own acceptance of all the Cari craziness that had been happening since then. Her sister was hurting and searching. Maybe this was what Cari had been searching for.

"I still think you might be crazy, but, at least, you have given your crazy some thought." And it did seem as if God was in the details so far. Who was she to stand in the way of that? "You do you, kiddo, but remember that while you are doing you, I will be doing me." Worrying, checking, double-checking, and then worrying some more. It had always been that way for her while they were growing up.

Cari didn't remember their father like Lacey did. Leaving him and moving to Marydale had been one of their mom's smartest decisions. It had not, however, removed Lacey's anxiety about keeping her sister safe. Time had lessened those anxious thoughts, and the house fire that had claimed her father's life had reduced them more, but she suspected she would always feel the need to protect her baby sister until sometime in the future, when she could entrust that task to the care of a good and godly man.

She had thought that Braydon was the man to take on that role. He had been all that a prospective husband should be, right up until he dumped Cari and he and his pregnant "second helping" got married the next month.

"I wouldn't want you to be anything other than you, sis," Cari said. "But you do know that your tendency to be overly uptight will not sway me from my plans, don't you?"

Lacey laughed. "If I have not learned that in the twenty-two years that you have been my sister, I doubt there is any hope of my learning anything."

Cari joined her in laughing. "We are a pair of opposites, aren't we?"

Lacey nodded. "But compatible opposites." Once again, she squeezed her sister's knee. "I'm glad I have you. Now, tell me where Emma lives. I only know the shopping part of Hatfield Falls and the directions to the community college."

"Take a left at the first stoplight."

~*~

Several turns and one complete turn around later, because her navigator was too slow in giving instructions, Lacey pulled her car into an alleyway and parked it in front of a garage. A dog jumped and barked at the fence in the yard across from where she had parked, but his tail was wagging too much to make him even faintly fearsome.

"That's Thor."

"You know Emma's neighbour's dog?"

"No, that's Emma's parents' dog. She lives in the apartment they just created in their old garage. They plan to use it as a short-term rental after Emma gets her own place."

"I see. So that's her parent's home?" Lacey pointed to the two-story white farmhouse.

"Yep."

"Does her place have room for two?" She would feel much better if she knew her sister was living so close to Emma's parents.

"Lacey, I'm getting my own place. Just as soon as I can find one that I can afford. I'll be fine." She swung her door open. "Now, put your you-doing-you on simmer and get out so we can meet Emma's brother. He has a few rental properties, and Emma was hopeful that he might know where I could get a good place for cheap."

"But Emma has room for two if needed?" Lacey asked as she climbed out of the car.

"She has a sofa bed if you need a place to stay on the weekend when I won't let you stay with me." Cari gave her door a firm shove closed to punctuate her sentence.

"Why wouldn't you let me stay with you?" Lacey teased. "I'm a joy and delight."

Cari shook her head. "And a pain in the neck – who

27

I love," she added with a smile before waving at the stairs next to the garage.

"Cari, Lacey! You're right on time. How punctual of you."

"Lacey wouldn't have it any other way." Cari cut a teasing glance in her sister's direction.

"Neither would Cari," Lacey retorted. "I was barely allowed time to make coffee before we left because my shower took longer than my sister thought was necessary."

"Come in. Come in. Will should be here soon. I told him 9:15 when I talked to him before bed last night, which means he should be here by 9:05. I wanted to give you both time to see my new place and use the bathroom before dealing with Will in the morning."

"Not a morning person?"

"Not a morning, noon, or night person," Emma said with a laugh. "Truly, he's a great brother, but I must warn you that he can be a naysayer and grumbler at times."

"You mean he sees the problems before they hit him?" Lacey gave Cari a look that she hoped said *"See. I'm not the only older sibling who tries to avoid issues before they become issues."*

"He often sees problems that could never hit him or anyone else," Emma retorted. "Coffee and cinnamon buns always help keep his *disaster is about to strike* love-liness at an endurable level when having to consider a new project – even if it is not his own project. And if we can win him over, Cari, I know he will help me convince Mom and Dad."

"I take it he's the responsible sibling?" Lacey asked.

"The responsible one that Mom listens to the most," Emma said with a shrug. "He thinks Edmund is Mom's favourite, but we all know better. It's him. He's too much of a Mr. Darcy for him not to be her favourite."

"Mr. Darcy?" Lacey asked in surprise. "Is your mother a Jane Austen fan?"

"To put it mildly, which is why my name is Emma."

"You're named after Emma Woodhouse?" Lacey wasn't sure she had ever met anyone who had been named after a book character before.

Emma turned to Cari. "The bathroom is the second door on the right."

"Thanks. I'll hurry, Lacey."

"Yep, Emma Woodhouse. That's me. Matchmaker extraordinaire." Emma laughed. "Do you know Jane Austen's works?"

"They're some of my favourites."

"Truly?" Emma looked impressed. "Then, having Austen fans as relations is something else Cari and I have in common." She motioned to the table. "I'll get the cups and plates. The buns will be done soon. I figured hot from the oven would be even better to warm Will's heart."

"I know it would work on mine. Those cinnamon buns smell fantastic."

"Thanks. They're Gran's recipe and Will's favourite. Well, they're all of my brother's favourite, actually, but Will has, shall we say, a more discerning palate than most of my other brothers."

"You mean he's picky?"

"Something like that."

Every time she saw Emma, whether in person or on a video chat with Cari, Lacey was struck anew with awe at the way someone so young could personify graciousness. It belied her age, for Emma seemed older than nineteen, or perhaps Lacey was just used to Cari, who had always seemed younger than her age due to her zest for life, as their mother had called it.

"You said you were named after an Austen character," Lacey said as she leaned against a counter in the kitchen. "What about your brothers?"

"Will is William for Mr. Darcy, though Mom wanted to name him Fitzwilliam."

A burst of laughter escaped Lacey. "He dodged a bullet on that one, didn't he?"

"He most certainly did. Then there is Brandon for Colonel Brandon, of course, and Henry, as in Tilney, and the twins, Edmund and Fredrick... Bertram and Wentworth respectively."

"One from every book?"

"All the novels."

"What would your mother have done if she'd had another child?" Cari asked as she rejoined them.

"There are always her juvenilia and *Lady Susan*," Lacey answered.

"Precisely," Emma said.

"I'll just be a moment." Lacey scooted down the hall while Cari opened her laptop and booted it up.

Lacey was just returning when she heard Emma greeting her brother. She paused, double-checked her hair with a pat of her hand, and then exited the short hallway into the living area. Emma was pretty so she knew that any brother of hers was unlikely to be unfortunate looking. However, she was not quite prepared for how beautiful a gentleman could be.

Will Bennett was gorgeous in his blue-striped, button-down shirt and casual but dressy sage chinos. Even his work boots seemed exceptionally attractive.

"This is my friend, Cari Welsh," Emma was saying.

Will's left brow arched, and his lips turned down slightly. Was the man disapproving of her sister without so much as speaking to her. That certainly took a sheen off his good looks. The jerk!

"And her sister, Lacey."

Will turned his pretty brown eyes in her direction and his skeptical eyebrow from a moment before, along with its less judgemental counterpart, rose in surprise.

"I didn't realize I was going to be meeting more than one friend." His eyes shifted back to Emma.

"Cari's car had to get its inspection today, so I offered to drive her down." Lacey swallowed her anxiety over having a disagreement for the second time since leaving her house today, walked over to the table, and took a seat. "I also wanted to meet the gentleman to whom I am entrusting my sister's apartment search."

Cari kicked her. Not that Lacey cared. This guy needed to know that he was not the only sibling who was skeptical of the new people in their sisters' lives. She could stand a kick or two, as well as Mr. Handsome's displeasure, if it meant keeping her sister safe.

"Will is the best," Emma said.

"I have no doubt he will prove himself to be so," Lacey assured her with a smile. But he did need to prove himself, and if he didn't, then, Cari was not going to be opening a café anywhere near his neighbourhood.

CHAPTER 3

"I'm happy to hear you have some confidence in me."
Will met Lacey's challenging look. What had he done
to earn this woman's disapproval? They had only just
been introduced!

She curled her pretty, pink lips at him. It was a pla-
cating expression of feigned pleasantness.

"Actually," she said, "I don't have any confidence in
you at all, but I have great faith in your sister. She has
proven to be quite trustworthy in all our interactions,
and she trusts you. Therefore, my trust is in her trust."

Her reasoning seemed a trifle circuitous, but he was
well-practiced in such logic since his mother seemed
to like to use it, and honestly, he couldn't blame Lacey
for being protective of her younger sister. It was a feeling he could most certainly relate to and admire.

"Then, you have placed your trust well," he assured
her.

Surprise flashed in her eyes.

"Emma is as honest as the day is long, as they say." He turned his attention from the feisty older sister to his own sister. "Your plans must be extremely non-mom-approved to require cinnamon buns." He raised a questioning eyebrow at her just as a small snort of laughter escaped Lacey.

"Have you been told the details of what this is all about?" he asked Lacey.

"More or less – although, I hope it's not less."

"Lacey knows most of it," Cari, said. "You will find, Mr. Bennett, that my sister tends towards being overly cautious. I can assure both of you that, while our plan is not as firmly developed as it will be in a few weeks, Emma and I have put hours into contemplating what we are proposing."

"Please, call me Will."

While Emma's friend sported a look that was not business-forward, she was well-spoken and seemed unafraid to tackle a problem head-on. Of course, he wouldn't expect his sister to have befriended a flake. Emma was too much of a thinker for that to happen. However, he had to admit that Cari's appearance had taken him by surprise. She reminded him a bit of a pink-haired sprite from a children's book. Neither she nor her sister was overly tall, but Cari's features were more delicate than those of her sister. That was not to say her sister was not attractive. She was. She most

34

certainly was – even when she was eyeing him suspiciously. It was just that Cari appeared more fragile.

"Will," Cari said with a smile, "I figured from what I have heard about you from your sister that you would appreciate a few figures and charts." She turned her laptop toward him and then clicked her phone. "This is so I can see what you are seeing," she explained.

"You have a presentation?" Apparently, the younger sister had not shared this part of the plan with the older sister.

"I do, and if you scoot over near Will, you can see it while I go through it."

Lacey looked at Will as if the idea of sitting next to him was one fraught with danger. She really did not trust him for whatever reason.

"Lacey," her sister whispered. "Please."

With a roll of her eyes, Lacey moved her chair closer to Will, and then, not seeming to be happy with the view of the laptop screen, she scooted even closer to him. Close enough that he could smell whatever fragrance she was wearing over the aroma of cinnamon buns. Whatever it was that she was wearing had a vanilla-like scent and actually mixed quite well with the cinnamon sweetness of Gran's cinnamon buns.

"Let me get you some coffee before Cari begins." Emma, who was still standing next to the table, hurried to the kitchen to grab the pot of coffee and two bottles of coffee creamer, one hazelnut flavoured and the other French vanilla, Will's favourite.

Once everyone had coffee and a cinnamon bun, Emma sat down, and Cari began her presentation. There were facts missing, but the basics of the concept seemed as if it could quite possibly be successful. Cari seemed even more of a thinker than his sister was – and that was saying something, something good.

"You may be able to help us fill in some of the figures that I have not yet been able to track down," Cari said. "At least, I hope you can since you have contacts in real estate. I know what the ads in the paper say for rents, but I do not know if those are accurate or if they are good."

"You're set on a storefront?" Will asked.

"What else would we have?" Emma seemed utterly surprised by his question. "We're not looking to do online sales only."

"In-person sales don't need a brick-and-mortar structure," Will countered while leaning back to enjoy his coffee and giving her time to reason that out. She would. He and she had always had these open-ended questions sorts of discussions over the years.

Her brow furrowed. "Are you suggesting craft fairs and farmer's markets?"

"Not directly, though what I was considering would make attending those possible, if you wished."

"You're not suggesting a food truck." Lacey's tone was not one that sounded receptive to the idea any more than her words did.

"I am." He sat forward and placed his cup on the table. "The start-up might be less expensive, and a mobile location could be spun into a social media campaign to gain customers and followers. Your sister and mine have said they were planning to start with a small menu. Perhaps it can be reduced even further to a handful of exceptional dishes – signatures, if you will." The low overhead was, in Will's mind, a great way to mitigate risk. Emma and Cari would be out a lot less cash if they found the business did not suit them or was not profitable.

Lacey shook her head. "It's not viable in the winter. What do you suggest they do to keep an income when the temperatures fall and the snow flies?"

"I'm not saying to *only* do a food truck. I'm saying start there."

"You expect them to have *two* businesses?"

She was looking at him as if he had sprouted horns or something equally as hideous.

"I thought your sister said you were the cautious, responsible sort," she said.

"He is," Emma inserted.

"Do you think what he is proposing is sensible?" Lacey asked Emma.

"I..." She looked warily at Will. "I am not certain yet, but maybe when he explains it all?"

"It's not a suggestion without merit," Cari interrupted. "Let me see if I'm seeing what you are, Will."

He waved a hand to let her know to go right ahead while he sank his teeth into a cinnamon bun. It would be good to know just how well the pink sprite could think. He needed to be able to trust her sense before he could endorse this business completely.

"You're saying start small. Form a menu that is maybe five items and can be cooked and stored in a small space. Then, test the concept at various locations in Hatfield Falls to see where our crowd is. It would be a bad thing to set up a café in a location that does not want what we are offering."

She was a smart cookie.

"We have from whenever we can get the permitting completed and the vehicle purchased and ready to serve food until probably December to discover where would be the best area to build our permanent location." Her eyes had started sparkling with excitement as she spoke. Apparently, his idea was taking root in her mind, and she liked what she saw.

"Neither Emma nor I expect this business to be our main source of income for a while. I have money put aside. Emma has this as her rent-free dwelling, and she has her education fund if she can access what won't be needed for her schooling."

Will grimaced at that. It did not go unnoticed.

"Community college does not cost what Bible college would," Cari said.

"True," he admitted. Cari most certainly hid a sharp mind behind her spritely image.

She smiled. "And if we are setting up in various locations, there would be a greater chance of Emma here meeting a mother-approved fella."

Emma gave an exasperated huff.

Had he said Cari's mind was sharp? He should have said cunning.

"We might even be able to find a few church events that we could provide catering for." Cari gasped. "Oh! We could even take advantage of the tourist season by being able to sell near cottages and beaches if we wanted – not now, but in the future. This could be how we start, but it could also be how we create more than one stream of income."

"Let's try to keep our focus on the present," Will said. He could feel Cari slipping into what he would call extreme dreamer mode. Nate was good at slipping into that state of being. Therefore, Will was well-versed in it.

"Sorry," Cari said with a grin that said she was not at all sorry she had found something to dream about.

"We do need to think about the here and now." Her eyes darted to Emma in what Will would call an almost sly look. "The future will see to itself – as long as we set up the present in the best fashion."

"I don't know, Cari. A food truck?" Emma said. "My mom is going to have a hard enough time accepting my not going to college as she wants me to."

"Mother will be an issue no matter what you are planning to do," Will said. "Trust me. I know."

"Is she not in favour of your land development?" Lacey asked.

"Oh, no, she thinks it's a grand scheme – her words." She was always using what he called Austenisms. "She just is an issue."

"How so?"

Before Will could do so much as draw a breath and begin to formulate a response, Emma was already answering for him. "Will is not married, nor does he have a girlfriend, nor does he seem to want a girlfriend, and worst of all, he will not name his development *Pemberley Shores*."

"Oh, that would be a lovely name," Lacey said.

"No, it would not be," Will retorted. "What is it with so many females liking all things *Pride and Prejudice*?"

"Do you have any idea how big the market is for Austen things?" Lacey asked in surprise.

"No, nor do I truly wish to know or be part of it. Now, back to Emma and Cari's plan. I'd be willing to invest in it."

"You would?" Lacey asked.

"As long as it begins as a food truck. Your sister has a good view of how using a food truck could be beneficial to creating the future they could have, and I would like to see the viability of the project before I invest too heavily if they need investors for future ventures."

Lacey picked up her cinnamon bun and looked at it from the top, then the side, and then the bottom. "What's in it?" she asked Emma.

"What do you mean?" his sister replied.

"You made it sound like your brother would be hard to convince about your idea to start a café. I assumed it was because he thought the idea was too extreme, too fast, too risky..." She waved her hand in a circle. "All that. And yet, he has been receptive and even countered with a more extreme idea. There must be something in the cinnamon buns. He has eaten two and become more agreeable with each bite."

Emma laughed. "I told you they were his favourites."

"Yes, but you did not mention magical qualities. He has gone from looking askance at my sister to applauding her ideas."

Will groaned. "Looking askance? Don't tell me. You like all that Austen stuff, too."

"She is quite fond of it," Cari answered.

"But not enough to name her children after the characters, right?" Emma's tone seemed almost desperate.

"Right," Lacey agreed before turning her attention back to Will. "What about housing for a student who is also starting a business? Do you have any clever ideas about that?"

"No, but I can track down some options that are both affordable and *safe*."

Finally, he had earned himself a look of delighted approval.

"I will need to know what she is looking for."

"A studio or bigger. I do not need a bathtub – a shower will do. I am capable of climbing a few stairs if needed. I have no pets, but I do have a sister who might want to visit. A patio would be nice, but no grass. I am not a gardener."

Will took out his phone and typed her info into his note app.

"Do you want it close to school?"

"It doesn't have to be. I have a car."

"Parking," Will said as he typed in that detail. "I assume the kitchen will be important?"

"Very."

He took a business card out of his pocket and handed it to her. "I just need to know how to contact you."

His phone pinged.

"You're quick," he said when he saw her contact information had been texted to him.

"I had the text ready," she admitted.

"You most certainly came prepared."

At that, Cari gave her sister what could only be described as a told-you-so look.

"You will need to meet my parents," Emma said. "Both of you."

"Both?" Will and Lacey said in unison.

"Yes. You know Mom, Will. She's going to want to know everything she can about Cari's family, so it is best if we just begin with the whole family."

"The whole family?" Will looked from his sister to Lacey. "This is your entire family?"

"We have an aunt, but she doesn't live here. She moved to Arizona last year because she was tired of the cold and damp weather we can get here."

"That's it?" They only had one aunt? No parents? No other siblings?

"That's it. Our mother died a couple of years ago," Lacey said.

"And our father died several years before that, not that we claimed him as family anyway," Cari added.

43

That was interesting.

"Our mother will want to know details," he cautioned. "It's how she is. She likes to know all she can about everyone she meets."

"Does your father know the pastor at Redeemer in Marydale?" Lacey asked.

"He does."

"It might be best if the two talked to each other. I will tell Pastor Anderson to expect his call."

Will's brow furrowed. Was there a reason Lacey did not want to talk about her family?

"From what Mom and Lacey have told me about my father," Cari said as if reading his mind, "he was not a nice person."

"I see. Then, I'll tell Dad to give your pastor a call. You don't mind if I do that, do you, Emma?"

"Not at all. I think I have enough to worry about with Mom being displeased." She smiled but it was not an all-encompassing expression.

"Hey, we'll convince her that you are not throwing away your only chance to be her one child who finds a soulmate at a young age," he teased her, causing her to chuckle.

"There is still hope for Fredrick and Edmund," she said. "They're not overly old. They're only twenty-four."

"That is true, and Henry hasn't hit twenty-six yet, so we will include him when Mother begins to moan."

"I don't think diverting her attention with our unmarried brothers will help much, but the thought is sweet."

"We'll convince her." He looked around the group. "Shall I suggest Sunday to Dad? That's when we all get together for lunch and tea, and it will give us a week to get things rolling. Cari might even have a solid lead on a place to live by then." He had a couple of places in mind for her already. One of them, he owned. He just needed to find out when the tenant was leaving and how much repair work would be required during turnover.

"You could come spend the night with me on Saturday and go to church with me in the morning," Emma suggested to her friends. "I can get Brandon to loan me a couple of cots, so you don't have to use the pull-out couch since it's dreadfully uncomfortable."

"I'm in," Cari said before turning to look at Lacey.

"Well, since I suspect I will still be between jobs, I suppose I can make that work." She did not look at all easy about the arrangement.

"It has to be done soon if we want our sisters to have the best chance at success," Will said.

She nodded slowly. "I know, but..."

"Yeah," he assured her. "I get it. I truly do." Letting

45

Emma live her life as an adult was not easy, nor was the thought of introducing his mother to two unattached women – one of whom liked Austen.

He stood. "Do you have a container I can put one of these in for later?" he asked Emma.

"I'll send one for Nate as well."

"No promises that he'll get it." It would be nothing to polish off both cinnamon buns later when he was ready for another cup of coffee.

"I'll put raisins in the next batch if you don't give it to him."

"You wouldn't."

Her look clearly said she would.

"Ok, you win. I'll make sure Nate gets a cinnamon bun." He turned to Emma's friends. "Are you in town for the day?"

"We are. I have a cooking class to instruct at *Friendly's*, and Lacey is going to find a quiet corner of the library to do some job searching from."

"My temp job just ended last Friday," Lacey explained, "and I'm hoping to find something more permanent this time around."

"What type of work are you looking for?" She had also risen from her place at the table, so she stood next to him. Her eyes were level with his shoulder.

"Office type work – receptionist, admin assistant, office manager – that sort of thing."

"Is there a good job market in Marydale?" It was not a terribly large town, so he didn't expect that there was.

She shook her head. "I plan to extend my search to retail if needed."

"What about looking for work in Hatfield Falls?"

She smiled and darted a look at her sister. "I'm not sure my sister wants me that close, but it is tempting."

"I thought it might be," he said with a chuckle. He knew that if Emma was his only family, he would be determined to be as close to her as he possibly could be.

"You do get it, don't you?"

He nodded. "Very much so." He leaned closer to her and whispered. "I can include two-bedroom places in my search."

She laughed. "She would kill me. She's quite determined to be on her own, and I have Mom's place in Marydale to look after."

"You own it?"

She nodded.

"You could sell it – unless it's too soon." Sometimes the sentimental value of a house far outweighed the market value.

"I may end up selling."

She did not look happy about the idea.

"Well, if you need help deciding what to do with

the property, let me know. I'd be happy to point you in the right direction." He grabbed the container of two cinnamon buns off the table. "It was good to meet you. Both of you." And with one last lingering look at Lacey, he headed off to work, though to be honest, he'd rather be going to the library and finding out more about Emma's new friend's sister.

CHAPTER 4

Lacey pushed the button with the wheelchair symbol on it and waited until the lady behind her had gone through the door before she entered. The breeze caught her hair and tried to tug it out of its ponytail. A seagull hobbled across the parking lot, stopping now and then to peck at what it thought might be food. I didn't matter that Hatfield Falls was twenty minutes from the ocean, seagulls were a regular scavenger one saw on the daily.

"You are a dear," the older lady said. "Thank you."

"Are you taking the elevator?" Lacey asked.

"I prefer it to the ramp, even if I do have a motor on this thing. There is just something about riding in an elevator that has been a joy to me since I was much younger and able-bodied than I currently am." Laughing blue eyes caught Lacey's. "Will you ride with me? The journeys of life are always better with a friend."

Lacey laughed. "I would have to agree."

Her new *friend* jabbed the elevator call button with the tip of her cane.

"I'm Barbara Green," she said as the elevator clunked to life and slowly made its descent to the entryway. "But you can call me Barb. The only one who ever called me Barbara was my mother."

"I'm Lacey Welsh."

"Lacey? What a pretty name! So much nicer sounding than Barb. I've never liked my name, but Barb is preferable to Barbara or Barbie." She gave Lacey a pointed look that said she truly despised being called Barbie. "I have a granddaughter about your age. A bit younger," Barb continued as the elevator doors opened, and she backed her wheelchair into the box. "You cannot ride in an elevator facing away from the door. It just isn't right," she explained.

"I'll try to remember that."

"I pray you never have a need to remember it."

"Are you going to the main floor or one of the upper ones?" Lacey asked.

"I'll start on the main. I like to let the librarians know I'm here." She chuckled. "Some of them are fun to tease," she whispered. "And excessively forgiving of an old woman. That's a perk of getting old and ending up in a chair – not that I can't walk," she added, lifting her cane. "I just can't do it for very long without becoming tired and my hip hurting like the dickens. What are you here for today? Work?" She nodded to the computer bag that hung over Lacey's shoulder.

"Job hunting," Lacey replied.

Barb looked her up and down. "Office work?" she asked.

Lacey nodded.

"I have a grandson who might be looking for an office administrator as soon as he discovers he can't do everything himself."

Lacey couldn't help laughing softly at that. "Control issues?"

"So many," Barb said with a shake of her head. "But with my daughter for his mother, it's no wonder he has a few. Amy is a lovely girl, but..." She grimaced and tapped her temple. "She gets an idea and there's no shaking her from it. Mostly her ideas are good, but a few are..." She paused as if not knowing how to continue.

"Enough to drive her son crazy?"

Barb chuckled and nodded. "That's it exactly." Again, she lowered her voice. "She does it purposefully because she loves him so much." She shrugged when Lacey looked at her and simply touched her temple again as if to say her daughter was not completely right in the head. "She takes after her father," she added, "but, ah, he was a good man."

The last part was said softly as the doors slid open and the main lobby of the library was revealed.

"Do you know a librarian named Edmund Bennett?" Lacey asked as she followed Barb out of the elevator.

Barb turned her wheelchair so she could look at Lacey. "I know all the librarians unless they have hired a new one in the last week. May I ask why you are looking for him?"

"His sister wanted me to deliver something to him."

"You know his sister?"

Lacey nodded. "I do. I met her through my sister, who met her at a church activity in Marydale."

"You're from Marydale, then?" She began slowly wheeling toward the information desk.

"I am. Cari – that's my sister – is in Hatfield Falls to put on a cooking class today at *Friendly's*."

Barb smiled. "I love those classes. Baking has always been my thing. Cakes, cookies, cinnamon buns..." Her voice trailed off as if lost in thought.

"Speaking of cinnamon buns," Lacey said, "that is what I am delivering to Emma's brother. They're delicious."

"If they're the ones I am thinking of, I'm happy to know you have also enjoyed them."

To Lacey that seemed an odd thing to say, and her expression must have registered her confusion.

"I taught Emma how to make those cinnamon buns," Barb explained.

She, this lady in the wheelchair beside Lacey, had taught Emma how to make the cinnamon buns? But that couldn't be because... "I thought the recipe for these was from her –"

"Gran! It's good to see you." A man, who looked to be about the same age as Lacey and had a strangely familiar look about him, greeted Barb with a kiss on the cheek.

"Edmund, dear, this young woman has something for you," Barb said.

"Edmund? Edmund Bennett?" Lacey's eyes flicked between Barb and Edmund.

"That's me. Have we met?"

"No," Barb said. "At least, not before right now."

"You're his grandmother?" she asked Barb as the connection was slowly forming in her surprised brain.

"I am. I am also Emma's grandmother."

Lacey smiled. "Then, I must commend you for the delicious cinnamon bun recipe. I've truly never had any others as good as these." She placed her tote bag on the floor, and, after sliding her laptop bag around to her back so it would not fall off her shoulder, she pulled out a container and held it out to Edmund. "Emma wanted me to deliver these cinnamon buns to you."

"Oh, are you a friend of Emma's?" Edmund asked.

"Yes, in a roundabout way," Lacey replied.

"Where are my manners?" Barb cried. "Edmund, this pretty young lady is Lacey Welsh. Her sister met Emma at a church function in Marydale and then introduced Lacey to Emma – or something like that." She paused and looked at Lacey. "Are you married?"

"No."

"Do you have a boyfriend?"

"Gran," Edmund rumbled softly.

"I'm merely curious," Barb said.

"No, no boyfriend, and I'm not looking for one either," Lacey answered when Barb looked at her expectantly.

"I like that."

"You do?" Both Lacey and Edmund said.

"I do." She shook her head. "The girls who only wish to marry and do nothing else have always annoyed me. It's not wrong for them to want that – I'm not disparaging. I just could never quite understand them. It will make our friendship better to know we're of a like mind on that."

Lacey looked from Barb to her grandson and simply smiled. She was not entirely certain what to say to such a thing, but it did appear as if she and Barb were going to be friends whether Lacey wished to be or not. Not that she didn't wish to be. It was just the way that

Barb had declared them friends from their first meeting that was a little unsettling. Lacey did not normally trust anyone upon first acquaintance.

"Lacey needs a place to plug in her computer and the Wi-Fi password," Barb said.

"There's a quiet room in the back left corner," Edmund said.

Barb cleared her throat.

"You know what?" Edmund said. "Why don't I show you where it is?"

"I'm sure I can find it on my own."

"No." He gave his grandmother a pointed look. "It is my pleasure to be of service, Miss Welsh. I would not wish to have a complaint lodged against me."

"A complaint?"

He nodded.

"You would complain about your grandson to his coworkers?" Lacey asked Barb.

"No, it's much worse than that," Edmund said with a wave of his hand toward the left of the library, indicating they should begin their journey. "She will tell my mother that I was less than a perfect gentleman to an unmarried lady with no boyfriend."

A burst of laughter escaped Lacey, drawing the attention of several library patrons and one library worker who grinned and waved to Barb.

"I'm a little fearful to meet your mother," Lacey said.

"Be thankful you don't have to," Edmund agreed.

"Oh, but I do. Probably on Sunday."

She had been uneasy about the idea of meeting the whole Bennett family and the conversation she knew was going to arise after that meeting, which might pit her against Emma's mother, but now her unease deepened. Mrs. Bennett sounded fearsome, and if she was anything like Barb... Oh, it was going to be an interesting meeting.

"You're coming to Mom's house on Sunday?"

"Perhaps. Will mentioned it."

"Will?" Barb said with some interest.

"He thought it would be a good idea for Cari – that's my sister –" she added to Edmund, "to meet the family since she and Emma are such good friends, and since I was there and am Cari's only family, he thought your mother would want to meet me as well."

"He did, did he?"

"Gran," Edmund scolded.

"I'm just interested in the story," Barb assured him. "Edmund, if you hear that Lacey and Cari are joining you for Sunday dinner, tell me. I want to be there for that."

"Gran."

"Can't your grandmother want to join you for a meal?"

Edmund gave Lacey an apologetic look. "You won't tell your sister to find a new friend, will you?"

Lacey shook her head. "Not yet. However, I think I want to reserve the right to change my mind until after I've met the rest of the family."

"The only one that might send you running is Amy," Barb said. "The others are quite reasonably normal. Now, where shall we sit to get this job-hunting stuff done?" She held up a hand. "I only wish to take a few notes on your qualifications so if I hear of someone who needs office personnel, I can direct them to you. There needs to be a computer available wherever we sit. I need to check my email on a proper-sized screen instead of my phone."

Edmund pulled out his phone and looked something up. "It looks like number fifteen has not been booked. You do know, Gran, that you're supposed to book the computers, don't you?"

"How can one book a computer before she knows she needs it?"

Barb's eyes were laughing again. She thoroughly enjoyed life, and Lacey had to admire that, even if she was not all that keen on having a job-search buddy. However, it might help her find a job faster than on her own, and it might even be one that would keep her close to her sister.

As much as Lacey did not look forward to the process of selling their mother's house in Marydale or trying to find her place in a new group of ladies at a new church, she did secretly want to live here while her sister did. She had told herself she would not, but if a job fell into her lap that required her to move, wouldn't that be God telling her that it was ok for her to follow her sister to Hatfield Falls?

"The password for the Wi-Fi is on the wall." Edmund pointed to a poster to the right of where his grandmother was parked in front of a computer.

Barb patted the space next to her. "Come, join me. Eddie will get cross if we shout across the room to each other."

"This is the quiet zone," Edmund's words to his grandmother held a warning, and Lacey wondered if he would truly ask his grandmother to leave if she broke the rules. He had been rather doting thus far.

"Whispering only," he added with a pointed look for Barb before he left.

Lacey sat down next to her new friend and began to set up her workstation. "Can we have coffee in here?" she whispered to Barb.

"Is it a spill-proof mug?"

Lacey held up her metal travel mug that Emma had so graciously filled for her.

"Then, you are fine. They only get testy if you pose a threat to the electronics or carpet."

That was good to know.

"I promise not to spill."

"If you do, I'll take the blame," Barb whispered conspiratorially. "They let me get away with a lot." She winked, causing Lacey to laugh and shake her head.

"Here," Barb slid a slip of paper across the table to Lacey. "Send your resume to that email address. I promise not to use it for anything other than my own information and to hand it out to a prospective employer if you allow me to do so."

Lacey eyed the email address.

"I worked in a doctor's office as a receptionist. I know lots of things that I cannot tell anyone else about. I can be trusted."

The way Barb said that last sentence – as if she knew that Lacey struggled with trusting new people – drew Lacey's eyes to hers.

"You have the same look a cat wears before it scurries under the bed," Barb explained.

"Do I really?"

Barb nodded. "I would bet you don't normally, but I can be a bit much at first and shake a few nerves." She laid a perfectly manicured hand on Lacey's arm. "But I am nothing compared to Amy."

Lacey sighed. Maybe she could find a way not to meet Mrs. Bennett.

"You'll be fine," Barb assured her. "Now, if you could send me that resume so I can read it and then post on social media about a friend looking for a job."

"You do not need to post about me on social media." She kept her social media profiles locked up as securely as possible.

"I won't use your name, and anyone who is interested will have to email me – provided they are friends who are well-acquainted enough to know my email address. I don't give that out to just anyone."

"We just met, and you gave it to me," Lacey argued.

"But you are not just anyone."

"I was until we took the elevator together, and I could still be. You don't know much about me."

Barb chuckled. "Emma trusted you to give cinnamon buns to Edmund, and Will is allowing you to meet his mother. That is all I need to know about you. There can be no higher recommendation except from God Himself." She chuckled again. "That was rather dramatic of me, was it not?"

Lacey could not deny that.

"The sooner I get your resume, the sooner I'll leave you in peace to read job-posting sites." Her brow furrowed and her lips pursed. "I wonder if they need someone at the library." She tapped on the keyboard. "I thought one of the ladies here was about to have a baby. It might just be a short-term job, but it would give Will time to discover he needs help in his office."

"Will?" Had she been talking about Will earlier?

Barb nodded. "He's just getting his new project underway. I don't think he realizes that he's going to need more staff than he has. I think you'd work well together."

Lacey laughed. "I don't."

"You don't?"

The thought of having to work next to the handsome and somewhat aloof Will Bennett – ok, so maybe he wasn't all that aloof, and it had just been a shaky first impression – but still, it was not the sort of job for which Lacey was looking.

"No."

"Why? You met him, right?"

"I did. Just this morning. It was not the best meeting in the world." Of course, it had not ended as dreadfully as she had thought it would when it began.

Barb's eyebrows rose at that. "What did he do?"

Lacey shook her head. "It was a look. I don't know, just call it sisterly instinct."

"Is that all? A look?"

Lacey could tell that Barb was not convinced, but

truly, she had nothing else to offer the woman about why she did not want to work with Will. She certainly couldn't tell Barb it was because she found Will attractive.

"I'm afraid that's it."

"Nothing else?"

"No. The look seemed judgmental," she offered quietly. "I'm sorry. I don't want to speak poorly about your grandson."

"You're not. Will can be judgmental at times. However, I don't think you should write him off as a possible employer just yet. Give him another opportunity to prove himself." She leaned closer to Lacey. "After all, he couldn't have been too critical of you or your sister if he is allowing you to meet the rest of his family."

She supposed that was true. Be that as it may, the idea of working with him was not one she was ready to accept just yet. "He also seemed rather condemning of a literary great."

"And who would that be?"

"Jane Austen."

Barb chuckled and turned back to her computer. "You like Jane Austen?"

"I do."

"So do I. So do I," Barb said. "But don't let me keep

you from your work. I will try to keep my distractions to a minimum."

And with that, Barb and Lacey fell into a companionable near-silence as Lacey scrolled through job postings and Barb chatted online with her friends, punctuating the chat with the occasional huff or chuckle.

CHAPTER 5

—⁓—

"Come in, son." Mark Bennett turned off his computer screen and removed his reading glasses when Will opened the door and poked his head into the church office. "Did you say hello to your mother?"

"Is she here?" Will was actually trying to avoid her. The fact that she was here was not going to make that possible. He'd have to go say hi, and then, she'd want to know why he was visiting his father on a weekday at church.

"She is. As are several other ladies. The nursery is being deep cleaned today."

"Ah, so that's why there are so many cars in the parking lot. I was wondering what meeting was happening that I hadn't remembered."

"There are no meetings today. That's why the ladies thought it was a good day to give the nursery a proper once over. They do it once a quarter, you know."

Will did know that. His mother had been doing her special nursery cleaning all his life.

"The janitor and nursery workers keep it in fine form," his father continued in his pastoral voice as if he were talking to someone who was not his son. "However, your mother insists that it gets more than a normal cleaning periodically."

"It is a good idea."

His father nodded and then smiled. "It is. Your mother, despite her oddities, is a wise woman." The comment was accompanied by a pointed look, and not one that a pastor would give a parishioner but one that was a father lecturing his son without saying a word.

"I know. I know." His mother was wise and loving and gracious and many other good things. "But her oddities drive me crazy at times."

His father chuckled. "Me, too," he agreed. "But I love her."

"As do I," Will admitted. He loved his mother as strongly as any son could, but he also wished as deeply as was humanly possible that she would let him find his own way in life without her suggestions for how to shape his future and find a wife.

"You know, Will, I never expected to marry someone like your mother. The lady I envisioned as my wife was a far more sedate woman with calm manners and guarded words." He shook his head. "I suppose such a lady fit the ideal of what one thinks of when one thinks of a pastor's wife, but I don't know why I ever thought such a woman would be a good fit for me." He leaned back in his chair. "It would have been a very dull existence to be married to a lady like that. Your mother is a perfect pastor's wife – at least, as perfect as a mere mortal can be. However, she is not dull."

A soft rumble of laughter rolled through Will of its own free will. "No, she's not that."

"She infuses this church's ministry with life."

That was true. No matter where Will's mom was, she brought life and light to the place.

"But," his father continued, "I am certain you didn't come here to hear me praise your mother."

"I don't mind it." In fact, he liked hearing his father speak so lovingly about his mother. He hoped to one day have a wife who would still captivate him after many years of marriage and children the way he knew his mother did his father. "However, I did come with a purpose."

"When do you not?" his father asked with a wink and a grin. "What can I do for you?"

"Emma has a friend she'd like Mom to meet."

"Does she?" His father's head cocked to the side as a look of curiosity settled on his face.

Will ignored the question he knew his father had. It

would be asked later. Right now, the basics about who this friend was needed to be shared. To tell anything more than that at present would jumble the facts.

"Yes. Her name is Cari Welsh, and Emma met her at an activity at Redeemer in Marydale."

"That sounds promising, but why are you bringing this to me rather than Emma talking to your mother?"

That was the question Will had ignored. "Emma is not planning to go to Bible college."

His father's expression remained neutral rather than showing the surprise Will expected.

"You knew?" Will asked.

"I didn't know, but I'm not surprised. Emma has never been excited by the idea of going to college the way some of you boys were. She is more goal-oriented and passion-driven. Taking a lot of classes that she would consider unnecessary to her goal would only annoy her." He sighed. "I suspected when she took a year between high school and college that she was buying time to find a way to tell her mother she had other plans. So, tell me, what are her plans? I know she must have some. Emma is not one to float through life without purpose. None of you are. And, I'll have you know, you have your mother to thank for that. She always kept you six busy and engaged in things you liked." He chuckled. "While also torturing you with a few things you did not appreciate. To build character as she always said."

Will shook his head. "Can you inform her that my character is built well enough?"

"No. I am not fond of arguing with your mother," his father replied with a laugh. "So, what is Emma's plan – a bakery? A café? A restaurant?"

"A café. However, I have suggested that she and Cari begin with a food truck to test both themselves and the waters of the market before they commit to any substantial business investments, like a building and renovations."

There was a hint of surprise in his father's eyes.

"Is that why Emma needs Mom to meet Cari?"

"Yep. That's it. She and Cari are planning to go into business together."

His father sat quietly for a few minutes and tilted his head this way and that as if weighing his thoughts. "Do you approve of Cari?"

Will shrugged. "I think I do." He had not thought he would when he had met her, but it hadn't taken long for him to realize that his first impressions based on her appearance were wrong. "She has pink hair."

"And you think her hair colour disqualifies her from being a good business partner?"

"No. I just think Mother might, especially when she finds out that Emma is not going to college to find a husband and is, instead, going to start a business with a pink-haired sprite."

Mr. Bennett laughed. "A pink-haired sprite?"

"I swear, Dad, she looks just like a fairy from some children's book. Petite, delicate features, pink hair."

His father continued to laugh. "I look forward to meeting this sprite. When do you propose we spring this on your mother?"

"You are truly ok with Emma starting a business?" He had thought his father might be the easier of the two to convince of the change in plans, but he had also expected a bit of push back about Bible college being a great place to immerse oneself in his or her faith while learning to be an adult.

"I am." His lips curled up on one side as if he knew he had confused Will.

"But you haven't met Cari yet."

"No, I haven't. However, you have, and I know you are very discerning. If it were Henry here telling me this, I might feel a greater need to discover things for myself, but you're not Henry. You're far more serious and thoughtful. I trust you. Not that I don't trust your brother."

While Will appreciated his father's trust, that comment both bolstered his spirits, as he knew his father meant it to, and weighed him down. Failure was not an option for Will. It never had been. His nature was not one that accepted failure easily, but every time someone as important to him as his father told him he trusted him, the more important it became to Will that he succeeded.

"I was thinking Sunday would be a good day. Cari and her sister could stay with Emma overnight and join us for church in the morning – or they could drive up from Marydale in time for church – and then stay for lunch and tea."

"Cari and her sister?" His father's eyebrows were lifted high in surprise.

Will nodded. "Emma thought Mother would want to meet Cari's family, and Lacey is the only family Cari has here. They have an aunt in Arizona, but that's it. Their mother died a few years ago, and their father died sometime before that. Lacey said to talk to Pastor Anderson about her father. She was unwilling to say more about him."

He was making a hash of this conversation. He had planned it all out in the truck on the way over here today, but now that he was into the discussion, everything just seemed to be tumbling out of him like balls out of a bucket when one of the kids knocked one over in the youth room.

"That's all I know."

His father's head was once again cocked to the side as he studied Will with what Will and his brothers had always called *the pastor mind-meld.* Henry had come up with the term after watching hours of *Star Trek* movies.

"Oh, and Lacey said she would let Pastor Anderson know to expect your call."

His father studied him for a moment longer and then took out a pen and notepad. "Then, I will call him."

"Does Sunday work?" Will rubbed his hands on his pants. Why in the world were his palms sweaty?

"It should. I'll check with your mother, but I can't think of a reason why it would be a problem." He looked up from writing his note about calling Pastor Anderson. "What is Cari's sister like? Her name is Lacey?"

"Yeah, it's Lacey." Will shrugged. "She is just a normal person, who is looking for a job and wants to make sure her sister is safe."

"No pink hair?"

"No; brown, normal hair." Which was much prettier than pink in Will's opinion.

"Not sprite-like?"

"Not particularly. She is not quite as petite and delicate as her sister." Though she was still petite.

"Do you approve of her?"

"I do." Probably more than he wanted to admit to. "I am meeting her and Cari in," he looked at his watch, "an hour to show them some apartments. Lacey wants to see what her sister's options are."

"Lacey is not moving here with her sister?"

Will chuckled. "I think she would like to, but Cari would not be overjoyed by it."

"But they get along?"

Will nodded. "As well as any siblings do. Or so it seems – I've only met her once." Which was just the number of times needed for him to know he'd like to meet her again, maybe multiple times. "She also has her mother's house in Marydale to think about."

"I see." His father's head was bobbing up and down slowly as if he were cataloguing all the information in his mind and the slight jiggling made it easier to do. "Do either of these young ladies have boyfriends? You know your mother will want to know that."

Oh, Will knew that! "Could you, please, try to keep Mother from pushing any of us at them?"

Mr. Bennett chuckled. "Only God performs miracles, son, but I will do my best. You know you could avoid her constant efforts to marry you off by finding a girlfriend."

"Dad."

Mr. Bennett held up his hands in defense. "I'm not pushing. I'm just suggesting a solution, and I will remind her not to scare off Emma's friends."

"Thank you." Will wiped his hands on his pants

again before rising. "I'd like to be able to tell Cari and Lacey the plans for Sunday as soon as you have them sorted out."

His father rose and came around the desk. "You're going to see your mother before you leave, aren't you?"

"I am." He knew if he didn't his mother would be upset, and, as much as she irritated him at times, he loved her far too much to be the willing cause of sadness to her. As he opened the door to go find his mother, he discovered her just crossing the foyer toward the office.

"I saw your truck," she said as she gave Will a hug. "Are you here to help clean the nursery?"

"No. I was here to talk to Dad."

His mother gave his father a curious look. "That's good because we just finished in the nursery, and I was coming to see if I could take Hatfield Falls' hottest pastor to lunch." She waggled her eyebrows.

"Mother, please."

"I would be happy to take such a lovely woman as yourself to lunch, Mrs. Bennett, but I have a question for you first."

"Do you?" His mother's eyelashes fluttered over surprised eyes.

"Would you be amenable to having guests for Sunday lunch and tea?"

"Oh!" his mother gasped. "Does Will have a girl-friend? Is that why he is here to talk to you on a week-day?"

"No," Will answered with a glare for his father that he hoped shouted *stop her!* as loudly as his mind was shouting it.

"Emma has a couple of friends she would like us to meet," his father said.

Mrs. Bennett's gaze shifted between Will and his father as if she were trying to figure out the connec-tion.

"From what I understand, neither young lady is married or attached," his father added. "However, I will advise you that if you are too forward in your desire to see Will or his brothers married, you could scare the pair off, and that would make your attempts to gain a daughter-in-law excessively more complex."

His father may claim that he was not a miracle worker but from the horrified look on Will's mother's face, there might actually be a miracle happening in front of his eyes, right here, in the church foyer.

"Oh, well, we would not want that," Will's mom agreed. "However, you cannot stop me from hoping. Will I like these young ladies?"

"They are Emma's friends. I have not met them, yet, but Will has."

His mother smiled as if she had been given the best

present in the world. "Would you care to join us for lunch, Will?"

"No. I'm not into hot pastors." He bit the inside of his cheek to keep from laughing at his mother's shocked gasp.

"You did say it, my dear," his father said. "And I am not going to deny it." He held his hand out to his wife. "Will thinks we will like both Miss Welshes. I understand one of them has pink hair and looks like a sprite in a children's book."

"Pink hair?" His mother's head whipped around to look over her shoulder at Will.

"Yes, but she is very bright and sensible," Mr. Bennett continued. "She has to be or neither Emma nor Will would approve of her."

"That is true."

"Her sister's hair is brown."

"Are they pretty?" she called to Will as her husband opened the front door of the church.

"Does that matter?" Mr. Bennett asked. "Are we to judge others on their looks?"

"No, we are not, but I would still like to know." She held her ground, despite her husband's attempt to pull her out of the building. "Are they pretty?" she asked Will once again.

Obviously, standing in the foyer and waiting for his

mother to be tucked away in the car was not going to keep him from having to answer a few questions.

"Yes," he said as he crossed to the door. "They are pretty, and I have just enough time to swing by my office and grab my lunch before I have to meet them to show them some apartments."

"Oh!" he heard his mother cry with delight as he dashed across the parking lot to his truck. "Are they new to town?" she shouted after him.

"Only one is," he called back.

"Only one?" There was a marked note of disappointment in his mother's voice.

"Of course, the other one might change her mind," he added quietly as he closed the truck's door and slipped his key into the ignition. And he would not mind if she did. However, there was no way on God's green earth he was even going to hint at that fact to his mother.

CHAPTER 6

—✦—

Lacey lowered her car window and turned off the engine. A pleasant summer breeze wafted in. It was neither too warm nor too humid today. In fact, it was a Goldilocks day – just right – which was excellent for apartment shopping.

The building in front of which she was parked, the first of several she and Cari were going to view today with Will, looked respectable enough. It was two stories high and appeared to be comprised of four homes – unless there were more steps leading to doors on the back of the building. However, since the parking spaces all seemed to be in front, and there were only eight plus two marked *guest*, she doubted this building had any more than the four homes she saw in front of her.

"I like the idea of outdoor space," Cari said, "but I had hoped it would be separate from the entrance."

"There might be another balcony on the back." A

covered porch ran the full length of the building on both levels with stairs coming down from the upper units on opposite ends of the deck.

"Then why would anyone have a barbeque on their front step if there is a place to put it in the back?"

That was a good question. Cari was referring, of course, to the apartment on the lower right, for it was the only one that had a barbeque amongst the items decorating the entryway. The one on the lower left had a lovely arrangement of flowering containers, and the upper left had two bikes hung by their tires from the roof that covered the deck. The upper right's entry was completely barren. That must be the unit they were going to view.

"I don't know," Lacey replied. "Maybe their baby plays on the back balcony? One front-step barbeque is not conclusive evidence that what you see here is all the outdoor space that comes with this place." She shifted to look toward the entrance to the parking lot. "What did Will say this one cost?"

As she watched for Will's truck, Lacey noted the enclosed bus stop that was just steps from the parking lot. That was convenient. Cari had a car, but having a second option for transportation was always good.

"It's in my budget. Just barely, but it's there."

"What amenities does it have?"

"Washer and dryer hookups. Heat pump A/C and

heat. Dishwasher. Bath and a half. And two bedrooms – so you can come to visit if you want."

Lacey smiled and turned her attention back to her sister. "We've never been apart for long." Except for when Cari had gone to college, but college was not permanent. This move could very well be.

"I'll be fine. You and Mom taught me well."

Lacey pulled her lower lip between her teeth and nodded. It wasn't that she feared that her sister was unprepared to be an independent adult. She was just not sure that she, herself, was ready to be on her own. Not that she could admit to that out loud. It sounded too needy, and not at all like she was the eldest sister. So, she let Cari think that her concern was about her being young and needing help.

"Who knows," Cari shifted so that her back was resting against her door, "Barb might find a job for you here –"

Lacey had told Cari all about Barb last night on their drive home to Marydale.

"—and then, you will be closer, and that second bedroom can become a massive walk-in closet with a plush tufted bench in the middle and a three-way mirror instead of a guest room."

Lacey laughed. Cari had always loved clothes. At one time, Lacey had thought her sister might own her own little clothing boutique, but, as it turned out, food had become a greater love than shoes and sweaters.

"You don't want me around," she said lightly, testing the waters to see how excited her sister was to be living away from her older sister.

"I wouldn't mind," Cari replied with a shrug.

Lacey blinked. She had expected something like "*I wouldn't mind having you around now and then*" as a response, not what amounted to an "*I'm going to miss you.*"

"Truly, Lacey, if Barb finds you a job here in Hatfield Falls, don't pass it up because you think I wouldn't want you near me. I don't mind if you are in the same town as I am and go to the same shops and church as me. I would, however, prefer for you to have your own place. You deserve it."

Lacey's brow furrowed. "Deserve it? What do you mean I deserve my own place?" Was that why Cari was moving out? So Lacey could have her own place?

"You need some time to not be a mom before you become a mom for real." Cari shrugged. "Between Mom and me, you have always had someone to care for. Don't think I don't know it – and I'll have you know that I knew it without your pointing it out to me."

"I like caring for people." Lacey pushed her door open as a gorgeous blue truck bearing the name *Ben-*

nett Homes pulled into the parking lot. She had always wanted a pickup, but they weren't practical or gas efficient. Therefore, she had never done more than admire the trucks on the car sales lot before finding the compact cars. The compacts fit her better anyway. She'd probably knock something over trying to park a vehicle as large as Will Bennet's truck.

"Then find a husband," Cari said as she also climbed out of the car, "and take care of him. I'd like to take care of myself for a while."

Lacey closed her car door and looked across the roof of the vehicle at her sister. "I know you do, and I'll let you, but I don't need a husband to do that."

"What do you have against marrying?"

"Nothing." When had her sister become such a matchmaking mama?

"Then, why do you not try to find a husband?"

Lacey bit back her retort of "*why don't you*" a moment before it was uttered. Cari, unlike Lacey, had tried to find a husband. It had just not worked out for her.

"What I need is a job," Lacey said instead. A permanent job this time. Preferably one that did not come with a boss who seemed to be fifty percent hands and eighty percent lecherous eyes.

"They're not all jerks," Cari whispered.

Lacey's brow furrowed.

"Men," Cari hissed.

"I don't think they are all jerks," Lacey replied. Several of them were, and Cari's ex was one of them!

"Then, treat Will like he's not one."

"As long as he treats you well, I will, but if he doesn't..." She ended her sentence with a glare.

"Ladies, I hope you weren't waiting long. I hit the construction on Elm at the wrong time." Will looked at his watch.

Did people actually still wear watches? Lacey couldn't remember the last time she had seen anyone below the age of fifty wearing a watch – a proper watch that is, such as Will was wearing. She had seen many people with fitness trackers that doubled as watches and even a few with a watch that doubled as a phone. The watch Will wore looked like it had one purpose – to tell time.

"I apologize for being five minutes late. It's not how I like to do business."

Lacey had to admit he looked a little flustered as he fiddled with his key ring.

"The unit I have opening shortly is number four." He pointed to the place directly above the apartment with the barbeque on the front porch. The very one Lacey had suspected was the apartment they would be viewing.

84

"Do the downstairs neighbours have children?" Cari asked.

Will gave her a wary look. "Are neighbours with children a deal-breaker?"

"No," Cari said with a laugh, "I was just wondering why there was a barbeque on their front step, and Lacey thought it might be because their baby played on the patio." Her voice lifted as if *patio* were a question, which Lacey knew it was.

"I'm not sure if the baby plays on the patio or not," Will replied as he led them to the stairs that would take them to number four.

Cari released a breath, and Lacey was just as relieved to know that the units had some outdoor space.

"However, they do have a child. Just the one, and they are the only current tenants in this building who do have children. There is an elderly couple in unit one and unit three is two brothers." He turned to look at Lacey. "Both in their mid to late twenties and friends of my brother Henry."

"Which means they are respectable, right?" Cari asked quickly as if she were afraid that Lacey would drag her by the ear away from a place that put her in close proximity to single guys. It was a valid concern.

"As respectable as any of Henry's friends are."

"And that is *respectable?*" Cari said the word respectable slowly, dragging out the syllables.

Will's brow furrowed, and he wore his wary look again. "Yes?" There was some uncertainty to his reply that made it sound more like a question than an answer.

"Are they single?" Lacey asked.

Will nodded. His hand with the key hovered near the lock on number four's front door. "Is that a problem?"

"I hope not," Lacey replied.

"It isn't for me," Cari said, "and I am the one deciding where I will live."

"I tell you what," Will said quickly as if he felt an argument was imminent, "they will probably be at church on Sunday, and if not, there's a singles night next Friday. I'll introduce you." He pushed the door open. "I vet my tenants thoroughly before renting to them. I didn't rent to Tyler and Blake just because they were friends of my brother, although that is how they knew the place was coming available when it did."

"This is your place?" Lacey asked.

"One of them." Will allowed them to enter ahead of him. "I flip a lot of the properties I purchase, but a few, such as this one, are better as rentals."

He closed the door and slipped off his work boots

– not the same pair he had worn to meet them at Emma's. This pair definitely looked as if they had seen several construction sites. He also wore a grey t shirt and some well-fitting blue jeans today instead of the dressier clothes he had worn yesterday.

"This tenant is in the process of relocating. That is why there are so many boxes and so little furniture. She's relying on friends to help her move in pieces to her new place. Of course, the whole apartment will be repainted, and any repairs will be made before you take up occupancy, Cari. Mrs. Garcia was an excellent tenant, but she has been here for a few years, so some things may need repairing or replacing just because of their age."

"How long was Mrs. Garcia here?" Lacey asked.

"I'm not entirely certain. She came with the building when I bought it seven years ago."

"Seven years ago?" How young had he been when he started buying properties?

"It was my first rental investment property purchase after I graduated from college."

"Bible college?" Cari asked with a grin.

Will nodded. "Business degree."

"And yet, you're not married." Cari's eyes twinkled with amusement.

"Much to my mother's disappointment, I am not." He waved an arm to the right. "The kitchen will have new appliances. These have not been upgraded since I bought the place. The other units all have newer, more energy-efficient appliances. Mrs. Garcia saw no need to upgrade, and she had decided that she was moving closer to her daughter right around the time I was going to start pushing her to accept the upgrade. Water is included in the rent, but all other utilities are the responsibility of the tenant."

A bar height counter divided the kitchen from a dining room that had a set of sliding glass doors to a balcony.

"These doors were installed two years ago. As you can see, there is plenty of room for a chair or two out here." He stepped out onto the balcony, and Lacey followed.

The balcony ran the full length of the apartment, just as the deck did in the front of the building, and just like in the front, this unit's section of the deck was divided from the next unit by a privacy wall. There was nothing to fault with this outdoor space. It was more than adequate.

"Do you think the kitchen will work for you?" Will asked Cari as he leaned against the balcony's railing and looked back through the open doors toward the kitchen. "I know it is more of a galley style than an open layout and, therefore, not quite as ideal for baking. However, I'm considering taking out that set of cabinets that divides the kitchen from the dining area and putting in a small island in its place. I think it would appeal to more renters that way. What do you think?" He turned his face toward Cari. "Would you find that to be a better arrangement?"

"Oh, yes! I definitely would," Cari answered. "How long do you think that would take?"

Lacey knew that a kitchen island was on her sister's list of things she wished for in a kitchen but was not willing to demand be there.

"I can have a crew knock that out pretty quickly."

A crew? That meant he had more than one, right? She knew that he had purchased land to develop, but until this moment she had not considered that his company was so substantial. She likely should have since Barb had said her grandson needed help, even if he was not willing to admit it.

"I'm sure it would be done before you moved in. Or nearly certain it would be." He pushed off the railing. "Of course, I have three other places to show you, and you have not even seen the bedrooms and bathrooms in this one."

"Are they all your places that you are showing us today?" Lacey asked as she followed behind Will and Cari.

"No, just this one is mine. The others would be commissioned finds."

He led them into a large bedroom that smelled a lot like Lacey's aunt's perfume.

"So you'll make money on this transaction no matter what I pick?" Cari poked her head into the closet.

"Yes, I will."

"More than adequate," Cari murmured as she closed the closet and made her way to the main bathroom that stood between the two bedrooms and contained a washer and dryer behind some old bi-fold doors.

"Those doors are getting replaced. That type of door is notorious for coming out of its track and being a bother to put back in."

"What are you replacing them with?" Cari asked.

"A barn door?"

Will looked at Lacey in surprise. "Yes. How did you know?"

Lacey shrugged. "It seems to be the thing to use in small spaces on all the shows, and what else would fit in here? A set of sliders would make it impossible to move clothes from the washer to the dryer and a regular door would need more room than is available to swing open."

His lips tipped up into a pleased smile. "You watch design shows?"

"Her favourites are the ones about tiny houses," Cari answered.

"Are they?" There was no mistaking the delight in his tone.

"I like how cleverly they're designed to make the most of the space." Lacey wasn't sure why she felt as if she needed to explain herself, but she did, and so she was. "I don't think I could ever live in one, but I do find it fun to see how others do."

"Hmm... You really don't think you could?"

Lacey shook her head. "Do you?"

"Yeah, I think I could. I don't need much space," Will said before turning back to Cari. "The second bedroom is through here. It has a half-bath attached, so not quite an en suite, but if it would make the difference between you renting and not renting, we could take a few square feet from the bedroom and add a shower. It would still be tight, but I think it's doable."

Cari had only turned halfway toward him from where she was once again checking out the closet before he added, "It might be done before you move in, but I'm not sure of the issues we might uncover. So, I can't make any promises. You might have to use the other bedroom for a few weeks and put up with some dust and noise."

"Are you saying my sister could be living in a construction zone?" Lacey wasn't sure she liked the idea of that, but it was not her decision. It was Cari's.

"I am," he said without wavering. "There would, of course, be compensation for doing so in the financial arrangements." He held Lacey's gaze. "It's beneficial to me as the property owner to make this apartment fit the needs of today's market better than it does now. Better properties equal better tenants and less turnover."

He smiled that disarmingly charming smile of his. "I don't tell all my prospective renters these things or ask for their input into what I am going to do with a place, but you're Emma's friends. And I know I would want to know all the details if I were the one helping Emma look for a place because I'd want to know she was in a good place with a landlord who took an active interest in his property."

"I'll take it," Cari inserted before Lacey could even formulate something to say in reply to how understanding Will was being. Wow, he was just the sort of landlord she'd want her sister to have, but...

"We haven't even seen the other three options."

"I don't need to see them. I like this place. Why muddle the mix if it isn't needed?"

"Are you sure?" Lacey wanted to ask about how this place compared to the others for price, but she refrained.

"I'm positive." Cari turned away from Lacey and

back to Will. "When can we go over the lease arrangements?"

Will looked as shocked as Lacey felt. "Are you certain you want this place? I mean, I want you to take it, but I only want that if it is the best option. The next place we were going to see is twenty-five dollars less per month."

Cari folded her arms. "And will that landlord give me a shower and a kitchen island along with fresh paint, new appliances, and," she looked down at the carpet, "new flooring?"

You could see where Mrs. Garcia had walked from one room to the next.

"If new flooring is all that is needed to sweeten the deal enough to have you take this place, then new flooring will be added to the list," he replied with a laugh. "But seriously," he said when he had sobered, "are you certain?"

"Absolutely, Will. It just feels like home." Cari shrugged. "And I won't have to share a bathroom with Lacey when she comes to visit."

"Well, then, I suppose I can have the papers ready by next week."

"That sounds perfect."

"Are you sure you don't want to see what you passed up? I have another three hours booked for apartment tours."

"Nope, no need," Cari was already on her way toward the door. "However, I'd love to see that new development Emma keeps telling me you are doing."

Will looked from Cari to Lacey. "There's not much to see."

"I'd still like to see it." And with that, she left the apartment.

"Does she always make such quick decisions?" Will asked.

"No. She's faster at it than I am, but this was exceptionally fast for her."

"Are you ok with it?" His eyes held as much concern as his tone did. It was as if it truly mattered to him that she was as happy with Cari's new place as Cari was. He was definitely not a jerk – even if he had appeared to be one at their first meeting.

Lacey looked around the living room. It was a decent place, the neighbourhood was one of the good but not overly pricey ones in Hatfield Falls, and Will would be a good landlord. Cari would have a good life here. She nodded. "Surprisingly, yes."

"And do you want to see the development?"

"Do I really have a choice?" Lacey asked with a laugh. "I'm sure you know how demanding little sisters can be."

"Indeed, I do." He joined her in laughing. "Indeed, I do."

CHAPTER 7

Will kept one eye on his rear-view mirror to make sure he did not lose Lacey on the way to his lot of land. She had typed the address into her phone's map app, but he still wanted to make sure she wasn't getting lost.

"You have issues, Will Bennet," he muttered to himself. He really needed to release his control on some things, and the fact that he was driving two kilometers per hour under the speed limit to make sure the car behind him would not get separated from him on a moderately busy road was an excellent example of that fact. His company was not getting any smaller.

The parcel of land they were now turning into was evidence of that. Soon, there would be twelve houses being erected on this land in addition to his own, which would be attached to the permanent office facility. He pulled into the make-shift parking lot in front of the mobile office unit he had rented.

Nate was here. His silver truck was backed up next to the door on the right, so Will parked next to him and left the better parking place on the left side of the door for Lacey. Hopping out of his truck, he motioned to the place where she could park.

Thankfully, she had seemed more welcoming and less wary of him today. In fact, he was almost certain that she was happy with him by the time they had left the Evans Street apartment, and he really hoped she was happy with him. It would make his life easier since he was going to be Cari's landlord and helping Emma and Cari get their business going.

Besides that, he liked Lacey. As in he *like* liked her. He chuckled to himself at how junior high that sounded, but it was an appropriate description. He'd even be open to asking her out if it wouldn't pose the risk of ruining Emma's dreams and plans should things not go well.

"So, this is it?" Cari asked as she got out of the car.

"I said it wasn't much to see," Will replied.

"But it will be." Cari stood looking down the gravel road the lot clearing vehicles were using. "How many homes will it be? I thought I had read a dozen?"

"A baker's dozen. I'll have a business office and home here that will double as the showroom while the project is under construction."

"You're going to live where you work?" Lacey

seemed shocked by that fact, but he couldn't tell if it was just a *how unusual* sort of shock or a *how ridiculous* sort of shock. Hopefully, it was the first type.

"It will help me get things done faster and lessen the need for on-site security, which will hopefully keep costs lower. Lower development costs mean more affordable housing."

She smiled at that. "That's right. I had read you wanted to keep these homes within the means of an entry-level buyer."

"Yep, that's the goal."

And he felt good about that. His business was about making money, of course, because one had to make money to stay in business. However, it was not all about making money and nothing else. Keeping listing prices reasonable and rents affordable on all his properties was his ministry to his community.

How many news reports had he heard or read about rents increasing beyond what some could afford? And now, the price to purchase houses was headed in the same direction. Something had to be done to stem the rising tide of costs. What he was doing was not a lot, but it was a start.

"It's an admirable goal."

And with those words from the pretty lady whom he *like liked*, he felt even better about his plans, because she did not seem to be the sort of person who threw her approval around willy-nilly.

"You can see from here where some of the trees are being removed to create room for houses. Not all the trees are being taken out. Just as many as is needed to do what needs doing. I'm not a fan of the knock everything flat and plop houses on an empty piece of land type of places I often see." He had climbed the two steps to the door of his office building while speaking and now held the door open for Cari and Lacey.

"Do you always do things your own way instead of the conventional way?" Lacey asked as she followed her sister up the steps and into his office.

"No," he answered. "Just when I think my way is better."

"Which is always," Nate said from where he sat at his computer.

"My friend and business partner, Nate Clark," Will said with a sweep of his hand toward his friend.

Nate pushed his keyboard away and slowly unfolded himself from his seated position. "The better part of the business. Ladies," he said with a nod of his head.

"Cari Welsh and my sister, Lacey." Cari had stuck out her hand to shake Nate's before Will could even open his mouth to introduce them properly to his friend.

"Ah, Emma's friend who is looking for an apartment."

"That's me, except I am no longer searching."

"You found a place already?" Nate asked in surprise, glancing at his watch. "I was wondering why Will was back so early. Which one did you pick?"

"The only one I saw," Cari replied with a laugh.

"I'm going to need a few guys to do some work at the Evans Street place," Will said.

Nate's eyes flicked to Will before returning to Cari, at whom he was staring slack-jawed. "You only saw one?"

Cari nodded. "Why would I need to see more than that if the one I saw was the one I want?"

Nate blinked and turned his attention to Will. Apparently, his amiable friend didn't know what to make of Cari's quick decision either. "You need a crew?"

"Yes."

"How big? What are we doing?"

"The kitchen, the half-bath, new flooring, new paint, and a barn door on the laundry," Cari answered.

Will shook his head. Her eyes were dancing with amusement much like Henry's would when he was being shocking.

"I'll get you a list of what needs to be done and by

when, and you can tell me if it is doable for your guys or not. If not, I'll call someone on my list who I've worked with before. However, I wanted you to have first refusal."

"Thanks, man. I appreciate it."

"Nate and I are partners on this project, but we also each have our own businesses outside of this," Will explained to Lacey who was looking slightly worried. "Nate often does my renovations for me, but he isn't always available. He just happens to be my favourite contractor to work with. Now, before I show you the plans for this place, would you like some coffee or perhaps a cold drink from the fridge?"

He was going to have coffee. It might be warm outside, but a cup of coffee was never unwelcomed to Will – not even on the hottest July or August day.

"Mugs are in this cupboard." He took one out for himself and placed it in the coffeemaker before selecting his favourite dark roast pod and dropping that in its slot.

Lacey had opened the fridge. "Wow. You certainly keep a selection of beverages."

Will chuckled as Lacey bent to look at the contents of the fridge more closely. "Nate keeps us supplied with those. He thinks you can only drink coffee in the months when you need to wear a jacket."

"Does he?" Lacey peeked over the fridge door at him.

The coffeemaker gurgled to life as Will nodded.

"Then, what is this?" She held up a bottle.

"*That* is not coffee."

She closed the fridge door. "It says coffee."

"You know what I mean," Will protested. "That is a coffee-flavoured beverage."

"Ingredients," she read, "cold-brewed coffee and other stuff."

He pointed to his nearly filled coffee mug. "Properly brewed coffee and no other stuff."

"No vanilla creamer this time?"

Nate chortled from his spot leaning against the kitchen sink. "I just put a new bottle in the fridge, Will."

"I saw," Lacey said with a laugh.

"Coffee should be hot."

"It can be, but it doesn't have to be. However, it's how I prefer it," Cari said.

There was another thing to like about Emma's new friend. She understood coffee, even if she did allow for cold coffee to be considered coffee and not just a coffee-flavoured beverage.

"I like it both ways." Lacey's words were punctuated by the pop of the bottle's lid. She took a sip. "Have you even tried this?"

"No." Why would he try a bottle of cold coffee that looked as if it had more milk than coffee in it?

"Then, you can't say anything negative about it," Cari said and shrugged when he looked at her. "It's not my rule. It's Lacey's." She smiled. "Aren't you glad you only have a little sister and not an older, bossy one?"

"Bossy?" Lacey cried. "I am not –" She stopped speaking and shook her head. "No, she's right. I can be bossy, but sometimes you have to be when it comes to little sisters. Am I right? Or am I right?" she asked Will. "Or maybe Emma is perfect," she added with a smile that was only partially hidden behind the mouth of the bottle she was sipping from.

"It sounds logical to me," Nate said. "Sorry, kid," he added to Cari, who thwacked his arm with the back of her hand. "Ouch."

"I'm not a kid."

"You are to your sister." He rubbed his arm. "How many rings do you have on that hand?"

She held up her hand. "Just one."

"One pointy one," he muttered.

"Sorry. I forgot about that."

"There's ice in the freezer," Will said as he took his cup of coffee and headed to the seating area they had set up for clients.

"I don't need ice," Nate grumbled.

"Roll up your sleeve and let me see if you do or not," Cari said. "I have first aid training, and I've fixed up more than one injury in a kitchen." She put her mug in the coffee machine, tossed in a coffee pod, and pushed the button to make it start gurgling. "Your arm."

"It's fine," Nate assured her.

Will chuckled as he watched Nate start to roll up the sleeve of his shirt when Cari's only response to his assurance was an icy glare.

"I'm not the only bossy sister. Cari can be demanding," Lacey whispered as she took the seat next to Will. "And she's not easily intimidated. She used to be less pushy, but things have changed with her in the past year."

"Is it something I should be concerned about?" Will had no desire to have his sister starting a business with someone who might be even the smallest bit unstable.

"Nah. She's relatively harmless. She's just sorting out who she really is after a few years of being who she thought she was supposed to be."

Will's brow furrowed. A person in search of her true identity did not sound like someone his sister should be starting a business with either.

"I'm sorry, but I don't follow."

Lacey smiled. "It's a long story that involves a jerk who dumped her."

"Were they dating long?"

Lacey's nodded. "Five years."

"Whoa."

"Turns out they were only dating exclusively on Cari's side of the relationship."

"Ah. Definitely a jerk."

"The world is full of them it seems." Her expression was slightly sad as she watched her sister examine Nate's arm before declaring that he was indeed fine and then asking him if he worked out or if his arms were so toned from swinging a hammer. Lacey shook her head as if she did not approve.

"Nate's no jerk," Will whispered.

"I didn't think he was." Lacey's reply was quick and perhaps a little defensive.

"I just wanted you to know that, in case your sister's flirting went any further than flirting." He rubbed the hand that was not holding his coffee mug on his pants. His palms were sweaty again.

Lacey grimaced. "I'd like to scold you for calling her a flirt, but I can't. She gets a little flirty at times, but she doesn't think she does. She says she's just being herself – which, to be honest, she is." She sighed and took a drink of her cold-brewed coffee. "So, this is a model of what the place will look like when it is finished?" She bent forward and examined the three-dimensional model on the coffee table.

"Yep, that's it."

"What name are you going to put on the sign?" She turned her head to look at him. "You can't just call it *this place* or *the development* forever."

He blew out a breath. "I know. I just haven't settled on a name for it yet." Every idea that had entered his head had never felt right.

She pressed her lips together as if trying to keep from grinning.

"Not that. I'm not calling it that."

She laughed. "Honestly, having seen this model, I think you're right not to call it *Pemberley Shores*. This feels less formal, and *Pemberley Shores* seems like a posher neighbourhood with a concierge and swim-up restaurants at two of the four pools or something."

"Thanks. Would you tell my mother that?"

Lacey shrugged. "If it comes up in conversation, I might, but not this Sunday. I think I'd rather not begin my acquaintance with your mother on a contradictory note."

"She's not so bad."

"That's not the impression I've gotten." Her phone buzzed.

"Go ahead and take it," he said when she looked at the screen to see who it was.

"Are you sure?"

He nodded. It could be a job offer. He'd hate to be the one to keep her from that.

"Hey, Barb."

Barb? His brow furrowed. No, it couldn't be his grandmother. There were lots of other Barbs in the world. Besides, how would Lacey know his grandmother? She wasn't from Hatfield Falls.

"No, we're not still looking at apartments."

Ah, it must be a friend checking on the housing search.

"Cari liked the first one we saw." She laughed. "You know that's just what she said?"

"Who's on the phone?" Nate whispered as he and Cari joined Will.

"Someone named Barb."

"No, I haven't found a job yet," Lacey said. "It hasn't even been twenty-four hours since I saw you."

"Cool," Cari said as she took a seat. "Ask if I can meet her," she whispered to her sister.

"You don't know her?"

Cari shook her head. "Lacey just met her yesterday at the library."

"Yes, Will's here. He was just showing me the model of *Definitely Not Pemberley Shores*."

Ok, that was weird. He didn't know anyone outside of his family and Nate, other than Cari and Lacey, who knew that his mother wanted him to call this place *Pemberley Shores*.

"Sure thing. Text me the address. We'll stop by before we go home. See you in a bit." Lacey held the phone out to Will. "Your grandmother wants to talk to you."

CHAPTER 8

Will took Lacey's phone and cautiously put it up to his ear. "Gran?" he asked as if he didn't believe that his grandmother was indeed on the phone even though Lacey had told him she was.

"You know Will's grandmother?" Nate's whisper was the sort that broadcast a secret rather than concealing it. She would need to remember to not ask him to share something that needed to be done discreetly.

"She met her yesterday at the library. Weren't you listening?" Cari fluttered her lashes at him.

Nate huffed and rolled his eyes. "It's shocking. Ok?"

"Sunday? How do you know about Sunday?" Will asked.

Lacey, who was still watching him as closely as one could when distracted by a second conversation, grimaced. "I told her and Edmund," she said to Will.

"You know Edmund, too?" Nate's whisper had grown a decibel louder. He was most certainly not the person to go to share things quietly – especially if that thing was in any way surprising.

"He was at the library," Lacey replied. "He works there."

"Of course, you can come," Will said. "I'll tell Mother."

"What's happening on Sunday?" Nate asked as he took a sip from his can of soda.

"We're meeting Will's parents," Cari answered with a grin.

Nate sputtered and coughed.

"We're meeting Emma's parents." Lacey shot her sister a look that she hoped told her to stop picking on Nate.

Cari shrugged and continued to grin, meaning the situation was likely hopeless.

"Emma and Cari are friends," Lacey explained. "That's how we met Will."

"I knew that," Nate muttered.

"Emma thought it was a good idea for Cari to meet the parents since they are..." Lacey stopped. She couldn't tell Nate that her sister was going into business with Emma. That was a secret until after Mr. and Mrs. Bennett had been told.

"Good friends," Cari concluded for her sister.

"And since Lacey is my sister, she got roped into the ordeal."

Nate shook his head, and an amused smile tipped his lips. "Do either of you have boyfriends?"

"No, nor are we looking for one," Lacey retorted. Although the man holding her phone was a tempting possibility if she were looking for one.

"Speak for yourself," Cari inserted before adding, "Actually, she's right. Now's not a great time to get into a relationship for me."

"I wasn't asking for me," Nate clarified. "It's just that Will's mother... well, let's just say she's anxious to plan a wedding."

Will swatted the air with his hand and the trio, sitting with him, fell silent.

"Ok, Gran, you can tell me about it later. I've got things to do, and Lacey and Cari can't leave until I've shown them my plans." Will closed his eyes. "No, Gran, I don't need that. Yes, I have things under control. I'm not going to lose my business because of mismanagement."

"Actually..." Nate attempted to interrupt Will but stopped when his attempt was met with a glare.

"I will keep it in mind. I promise. If things start to crumble, I will hire someone."

Oh, dear! Lacey's heart began to race. Was Barb trying to get Will to hire her?

"Yes, I can afford to do that. Send me what you have, and I will file it."

Lacey groaned silently. If her thoughts were running in the right direction, her resume was going to end up in Will's inbox. Talk about looking desperate!

"Love you, too, Gran." Will clicked the end call button and passed the phone back to Lacey.

"Everything ok with your gran?" Nate asked.

Will nodded. "She's just at me again to hire some office help."

"It might not be a bad idea," Nate said.

Will's brow furrowed. "Why? We've got things under control, don't we?"

Nate grimaced. "I thought we did, but I received a call when you were out. I didn't want to bother you with it until your appointments were over, so I put the message on your desk rather than texting."

Will looked at the model on the table and then towards his desk, seemingly torn between doing what he had planned and finding out what the issue was that Nate was not sharing.

"We're ok on our own if you two want to go discuss whatever it is," Lacey offered. "Don't let my sister's curiosity about your building plans hold you back from conducting business."

"No, no. I said I would show you the development, so let me do that. I'm assuming whatever it is can wait since Nate wasn't going to tell me about it until later anyway." He shot a questioning look at his friend.

Nate nodded. "Municipal offices are open later today."

Will's hand stilled over the brochure that sat next to the model on the table.

"Go, discuss it," Lacey urged him. "Anything that involves the municipal offices probably shouldn't be put off."

"He just needs to sign a form and get it in before they close," Nate said.

"That form isn't due until Friday," Will said.

Nate shook his head. "Sorry, but the person who called me said that the wrong date was on the form. I guess she's an intern working with them this summer to earn college credits, and she got the wrong date. I tried to talk her into an extension, but she said that with various people taking vacations, her hands were tied."

Will had the brochure in his hand now, but he looked totally flummoxed about what to do. Lacey took out her phone and opened the search app.

"You just have to sign it and drop it off, Will. It's no big deal," Nate assured him.

"You're certain their offices are open late today?"

Nate assured Will that they were open until either

six or eight on Tuesdays just as someone on the other end of Lacey's call picked up.

"Hello. This is Lacey Welsh. I was wondering if you could tell me what the latest time is that I can drop off papers today and have them marked as received on time?"

All eyes turned towards Lacey.

"We're open until seven on Tuesdays," the woman on the other end of the phone answered.

"And there will be someone at the desk to receive papers from now until seven? No one will be taking a dinner break?" How many times had she attempted to get something done on time for an employer and run into the inconvenience of having to wait for someone to finish their lunch? She'd rather that Will be able to avoid that annoyance if possible.

"Actually, I'm the one who is on for the evening shift this week, so I can guarantee you that there will be someone here. I take it that these forms are important and time-sensitive?"

"Yes, ma'am, they are."

"Call me Doreen. Ma'am makes me feel as old as I am. Whom should I be watching for?"

"Will Bennett. He'll be there well before seven. In fact, my guess is that he'll be there just as soon as he can be, but I wanted to cover all the bases in case he gets delayed."

"Ah, yes, I have a note here that Will Bennett might be dropping off some permit forms. I'll keep an eye out for him."

"Thank you, Doreen. He'll be happy to hear it." Lacey ended the call and put her phone in her lap. "You have until seven, and Doreen will be watching for you." Was it warm in here? She was feeling decidedly warm. Perhaps, from the surprised expression Will wore, she shouldn't have tried to solve this problem for him.

"Sorry," she muttered, letting her eyes drop to the model in front of her. "I was just checking the time they closed. I didn't expect to have to answer questions about who would be dropping off the papers."

The room sat silent for a moment before Nate cleared his throat. "Thanks for the backup." He smiled at her when she glanced his way.

Lacey shook her head. "I'm sorry. Really, I am. It wasn't my place. I just..." She shrugged. How did she explain that the thought of men possibly raising their voices and arguing sometimes made her panic and look for a way to fix things?

"Lacey is great at taking care of things," Cari explained. "She always has been."

"I can see that." Will seemed to have finally found his voice. "Thank you."

"I'm sure Nate had all the information you needed, I..." Again, she was lost for words.

"Seriously, thank you. I would have been uneasy until I had looked up the hours myself."

"That's the truth," Nate agreed, "Will rarely takes anyone's word on something without double-checking. Now, Miss Welsh, can you help me get an invite to lunch at the Bennett house on Sunday?"

Will shook his head and chuckled. "You're not getting one, but I'm supposed to extend an invitation to Cari and Lacey to join us on Sunday. I just hadn't gotten to that yet. Both Dad and Mom seem eager to meet you."

Nate laughed. "Eager is likely an understatement when it comes to your mother." He turned back to Lacey and Cari. "As I was saying, she's eager to see her sons married off."

Will sighed. "They already know that. Emma warned them."

"So did your grandmother and brother," Lacey said.

"Did they?"

Lacey nodded. "Not in so many words but yes."

"Then, it sounds as if you have been thoroughly warned," Nate said with a laugh.

"I have been." And yet, she was still going to meet

Will's mother because it was just what she had to do for her sister.

"Is this actually how each house is going to look?" She motioned to the model as she brought the conversation back to where it should be. They were in Will's office to see the plans for the development he was building, after all. They were not here to consider why a guy as handsome as Will Bennett was not yet married or even dating.

She had determined that he was not a jerk – a bit uptight perhaps, based on how he had spoken to his grandmother and how Barb had spoken about him – but he was not a jerk. In fact, he appeared to be a man with a loving heart – was he not building this subdivision to serve those in need of affordable housing, and had he not gone out of his way to make sure both she and her sister were comfortable about the apartment he had shown them? So then, what was it? What kept him from being taken?

"I'm sorry. Could you repeat that?" She tore her eyes away from studying the way his mouth moved and focused on listening to the words coming out of it.

"We have plans for all of these, and this is how it will look unless someone purchases before the house is built and wishes to pay for limited customization." He handed her the brochure he held. "These are the options that will fit within the price range for any house on any lot.

"The lots closer to the lake will be slightly higher in price as they will be the most desirable, but even so, their price will not go over the top price listed there. I want these houses to remain affordable, though I know once they have been purchased, I can't stop someone from adding value, nor can I control what tax assessments will do."

"But we want to start with each place being affordable," Nate said.

"Oh, I like that!" Cari pointed to a bedroom with a large walk-in closet. "These are all made from containers?"

"With some stick frames added here and there to join things together," Nate replied.

"I thought they would all be long and narrow."

"You'd be surprised what can be done with a few containers," Lacey said.

"You know about container homes?" Nate asked.

"She watches home design shows." Will's voice held that hint of delight it had at the apartment when she knew about what kind of door he was going to hang for the laundry.

"Cool. I like watching those, too. Or I like many of them." Nate's phone buzzed. "Oh, that's my reminder that I have a client appointment today. They want a kitchen remodeled. Ladies, it was a pleasure to meet you."

"I'll email you the scope of work for the Evans Street apartment after I get the papers submitted," Will called after Nate.

"I'll be looking for it." He unplugged his laptop and put it in his bag, before grabbing his keys and heading out the door.

"We should probably go, too," Lacey said. "Barb will be waiting."

"Her cookies are good," Will said. "She told me she was just getting some out of the oven and waiting to share them."

"Are they as good as her cinnamon buns?" Cari asked.

Will shook his head. "Almost but not quite. Not that I'm saying they're deficient. I'm just saying those cinnamon buns are hard to beat."

Lacey couldn't argue with that.

"Do you have a bathroom?" Cari asked. "One that isn't a blue plastic hut?"

Will chuckled. "That door." He pointed to the other end of the long office building.

Lacey started gathering their beverage containers from the coffee table.

"I can do that," Will said, jumping up.

"I don't mind doing it." And she didn't. She liked having something to do.

"Well, at least, let me help you." He took Cari's cup from her. His fingers brushed hers in the exchange while his eyes held her gaze for an intense minute. Then, he blinked and picked up his own cup. "I'll put these in the dishwasher. You can put those in the recycling." He glanced at her again, and the right side of his mouth tipped up as if he had landed on a happy thought but wasn't entirely certain if he should be completely happy or not.

Together they walked over to the kitchen.

"Do you drink real coffee?" he asked when they were standing side by side at the sink as he rinsed his cup and she waited to do the same with the containers she held.

Lacey laughed and held her empty bottle in front of him. "I did today."

"You know what I mean." He pulled open the dishwasher and put one mug in while Lacey rinsed Nate's can and tossed it in the blue bin, following it with her bottle.

"Yes, but I prefer cold coffee in the summer."

"I suppose a coffee shop sells that, right?" With the second mug still in his hand, he turned to look at her.

"They do." She stood empty-handed, leaning one hip against the sink as she faced him.

"Would you like to go out for coffee with me some-time?"

Her eyes popped open wide. "Like on a date?" She had not expected that. Not that she was unpleasantly surprised. She was quite the opposite.

He shrugged and looked away but just for a moment. "I thought we should get to know one another better since we need to make sure our sisters are ok, ya know?"

"Oh, so more like a strategy meeting?" And not a date? That was disappointing. She knew she had said she was not looking for a boyfriend, but if one as handsome as Will Bennett was dropped in her lap, she was not going to say, *"No, thank you. I'll wait for the next one."*

He took his time putting the mug he held in the dishwasher. "A strategy date?" He tore off some paper towels and dried his hands. "What do you think?"

She wasn't sure what to think. What in the world was a strategy date? "Sure, we could do that."

"I was thinking we could meet at the coffee place in Marydale – the one just down from the high school. Maybe on Friday afternoon?"

"That could work." She handed him her phone. "I'll need your number in case something comes up, and I'd rather not ask Cari for it."

He took her phone and handed her his. "Good idea.

We should probably keep this quiet for now – especially where my mother is concerned." He paused in the process of typing in his number. "It's not that I'm embarrassed to go out with you or anything." He blew out a breath. "It's just my mother."

"I get it. My sister has been pushing me to date someone – anyone." She smiled to try to alleviate the awkwardness she was feeling. "But this is just a strategy date so no need to get her hopes up or anything. Right?"

His eyes held hers for a moment. Then, she saw his throat move up and down as if swallowing before answering her. "Right. It's just a strategy date for now."

For now? Did she dare hope he meant that any further dates might be worth getting her hopes up over?

He handed her phone back to her just as she heard the bathroom door open, and the fan shut off.

"Text me the time," she whispered as she shoved his phone across the top of the kitchen counter in his direction.

"Will do." He pocketed his phone. "I suppose I need to get those papers signed and delivered." He walked with her to the door. "Thanks again for calling to check on hours so I didn't have to. It saved me some stress and time. I really do appreciate it." He held the door open for them as they exited. "Eat a cookie for me."

CHAPTER 9

Will checked his reflection in the small mirror in the office bathroom. "It's just coffee," he said to himself. "You can do this."

He washed his hands for the third time to remove the sweat from them. It was a pointless effort, but he did it anyway. His nerves were as much on edge today as they had ever been. In fact, he wasn't sure he had felt this anxious about anything since he had given the valedictorian speech back in high school.

Still clutching a sheet of paper towel, he left the bathroom and went to gather his things from his desk. The tiny green light on his phone blinked off and on, off and on. He dried his hands once more, tossed the towel into the metal waste can next to his desk, and unlocked his phone's screen to find a text from Lacey.

I can't meet you today. I have an interview!

Will dropped into his desk chair. All this worrying, fidgeting, and being unable to focus on a single task today had been for nothing? Worse, it would have to be repeated at some point.

"Bad news?" Nate asked.

"A meeting needs to be rescheduled," Will answered.

"Ah, schedule changes – one of your favourite things." Nate's smile was understanding, if somewhat amused.

Will did like to stick to a schedule as much as possible, but the fact that his schedule had been rearranged was not the thing that had him fighting disappointment. Despite his nerves, he had been looking forward to this date. It would have been his first one in five years. There hadn't been anyone who had appealed to him enough to risk dating and having his mother find out. And it *was* a date, even if he had backpedaled some and called it a strategy date. What was a strategy date anyway? He shook his head.

Where's the interview?

Hopefully, it was in Hatfield Falls and he would need to help Lacey find an apartment – but not because he would make some money in the process. He would do this one for free if he had to. Marydale was only forty-five minutes from Hatfield Falls, but it, and Lacey, *were* forty-five minutes away from Hatfield Falls.

There's a temporary opening at the Hatfield Falls library.

Barb gave me the forms to fill out when we stopped by for cookies. ?

A smile leapt to Will's lips. That was great news! It was a possible job in Hatfield Falls. She would be closer to him if she got this job.

Want to meet after the interview before you head home? My schedule is pretty clear today.

He drummed his fingers on his desk and blew out a breath as he waited.

Cari is planning to come with me so she can visit Emma. Sorry.

Well, that was that.

No problem. Things happen. It's too bad though.

He reread the words. They were casual but expressed disappointment. Was it enough to let her know that he was interested in her more than a date labelled as a *strategy date* indicated? Deciding they might not be, he added *I was looking forward to it*. Then, he pressed send.

Her reply was quick in coming. *Me, too.*

Will spun his chair so that Nate would not see his small fist pump and mouthed "Yes!"

It's great about the interview. Hope it goes well. Can we reschedule? After your interview. Don't bother with thinking about rescheduling now.

If they rescheduled now, there wouldn't be a need for her to text or call him later.

Does it need to be before Sunday?

He shook his head as he typed, *Need isn't the word. Want would be better. But no, we can do it next week, too.*

"That's a lot of dinging," Nate called across the room. "Makes it hard for a fella to get his work done."

"Shut up," Will shot back, causing Nate to laugh.

"Just seems it shouldn't take quite so long to reschedule an appointment."

"Sometimes it does." Especially when the appointment was a date.

Ok. I'll let you know what looks best later. I need to head out. It would be bad to be late for this.

Yes, that would be bad.

Let me know how it goes. Saying a prayer for success now. Thanks. TTYL

Will sat with his back to Nate for a minute just looking at his silent phone and praying as he had said he would.

"Got it all sorted out?" Nate asked.

Will shook his head. "They need to check their schedule. So, they'll get back to me." He pushed up from his seat. "I guess that means I can go check on the progress of the house on Tulip."

"It was looking good yesterday," Nate said. "I helped them carry in the countertops."

"The countertops came early?"

"No, they were a day late."

Will opened his calendar. "This says they were to arrive today, which is why I had planned to stop by there."

"The receipt said yesterday's date when I signed off on it."

"Are you sure?"

"Positive."

"Huh. I wonder how I got that confused?" He had never missed a scheduled delivery before, and he wasn't sure how he had managed to miss this one. As he was attempting to decipher where he had made his mistake, his phone buzzed.

"Will Bennett."

"Mr. Bennett, this is Doreen from the city. We met on Tuesday. I'm afraid I have some news for you that you're not going to like. It seems your submission was missing a page. Now, it's not your fault. We failed to send it to you, but it is going to delay your permit by, at least, two weeks."

Her words hit him like a punch to the gut. How had he not noticed that a page was missing? He shook his head. That made it two errors that had been brought to his attention in as many minutes and neither one was insignificant. Both had the potential to delay projects. This current error already promised a small delay. "Two weeks, you say?"

"Yes, Mr. Bennett. That is the fastest I can hope to

get these papers through the system, and that's only if you can pick up the form you need today and return it by Monday."

"Today?"

"Yes, sir. I'll be at my desk for two more hours. I can leave this with Charlie when he comes in, but I'd really like to be able to apologize to you in person."

It seemed he'd be stopping at the municipal offices instead of going to Tulip to see if the countertop was up to standard. "Does the missing page need more than a signature?"

"I'm afraid it does. There are a few numbers and other details to fill in. You're welcome to do that here if you have all the information with you that is needed, and that would get this ball started rolling a little bit faster."

Will sat down at his desk. "I'm putting you on speaker so I can jot down what you tell me I need." Then, he pulled out a pad of paper and scribbled down the three things she told him. "I'll be there in half an hour with what is needed."

"I am terribly sorry for the inconvenience, Mr. Bennett. See you when you get here. Just pop to the front of the line, and I'll have the paper ready for you."

He thanked her and then hung up.

"What was that about?" Nate asked.

"There was a page missing from our application."

"I don't remember noticing a missing page." Nate's words soothed Will's mind somewhat. At least, he was not the only one to have missed that page.

"Nor do I, but I know I also did not fill in the information she just told me she needed."

Nate pulled a binder from the shelf next to his desk and flipped it open. "This has everything you'll need." He flagged three pages with colourful sticky notes shaped like arrows. "I guess your visit to Tulip will have to wait."

"I guess so. But you said it was looking good, right?"

"Yep. Totally up to standard – yours and mine."

"I wouldn't expect less, but..."

"Yeah, I know. You like to see it with your own eyes. I guess you're just going to have to trust me this time."

Will nodded slowly. "I guess so."

Trusting anyone when it came to seeing a project completed as he wanted it to be done was not easy for Will – not even when it was his best friend whom he was being called on to trust. Of course, not easy did not mean impossible. Or so he told himself as he rose from his chair again.

"Did the floor stain look like it was going to complement the countertops?" He had been waiting to get those countertops in before he decided on the stain.

"It looked great. Should I tell my guys to start the

floors before they leave tonight? If so, we could have this one wrapped up earlier than expected."

"You're sure it looked good?"

Nate nodded. "You know you don't have to have your hand in every little detail, right?"

Will sighed. "I know."

But he felt that if he didn't and the project failed – which, in this case, failure was the house selling for less than they needed it to – it would be his fault for not paying closer attention to details. He knew he could not control the housing market and what buyers were willing to pay for a place, but somehow, knowing that he had put in his best effort and had touched every detail, made the sting of a lower profit smart less.

"Tell them to go ahead." Today, he would trust Nate and keep his fingers off this detail. After all, Nate had as much to lose on this project as Will did. It was their first fifty-fifty split of the investment in the house and the profit coming out of it.

"Will do, boss."

"Partner," Will corrected.

"Yeah, boss, partner, it's kind of all the same."

Will stopped at the door. "Do you really feel like I'm your boss?"

Nate shrugged. "You do like to think your way is the only way."

Wow. That stung. "I'm sorry."

"It's just how you are, and honestly, you're right most of the time. So, that makes it easy for me to let you be the boss."

That really did not lessen the sting Will's pride was feeling. "I'll work on it," he promised quickly before ducking out the door.

He had reached his pickup before he realized that the binder he needed was still on Nate's desk.

"Missing something?" Nate called from the steps when Will closed the truck's door to return to the office.

That was a loaded question. It seemed that Will was missing a lot of things lately. Perhaps Gran was right. Maybe he did need to hire some office help. With the binder he needed safely stowed in the compartment between the seats of his truck and with the worry that he might not be able to keep up with the work he had set before himself niggling at his mind, Will pulled out of the parking lot and headed towards the town's centre.

~*~

Will stepped back out into the late afternoon sunshine. The paper that had needed attention had been attended to and submitted. He'd watched Doreen place it securely in the folder with the other papers. Now, it was just a waiting game to see if anything else would be required of him and Nate before their permits would be granted.

He could really use a cup of coffee and something sweet. The combination of the missed details, Nate's words about not feeling like a partner, and spending an hour and a half in an uncomfortable chair, filling out forms and waiting to submit them, had left Will's equanimity beyond shaken. It needed a balm of some sort, and coffee and sweets seemed like a good prescription.

He'd really rather not go by himself, because a distraction from his thoughts would be beneficial. He looked across the parking lot to the library. Maybe Edmund would like to join him. His lips tipped up and his mood lightened. Maybe, just maybe, in the process of seeing if Edmund was able to go with him, Will might run into Lacey. Seeing her might be even better than coffee and cinnamon buns.

He stashed the binder he held back in the compartment in the truck's center console and took two steps toward the library before stopping. If he had too much going on in his life now to keep on top of things, did he really have time and space for a relationship?

"Will?"

He spun to find his grandmother rolling up to him in her wheelchair.

"What are you doing here?" she asked. "And why are you standing there staring at the library?"

"I was just taking care of some paperwork." He tilted his head towards the city offices. "And then, I was thinking about getting coffee and thought I would see if Edmund wanted to join me."

"He works until five today."

It did not surprise him that his grandmother knew Edmund's schedule. Gran lived a good part of her life at the library, especially during the summer when she did not need to rely so heavily on the accessible bus schedule. If there was such a thing as a winterized wheelchair, she'd likely have bought one. She could drive, and she had a car. However, it was still challenging for her to go anywhere where she might have to be on her feet for very long.

"Are you ever going to have that hip surgery?" Will asked her.

"In January."

"Really? You have a date?" She had been adamant that she did not need a new hip ever since the doctor had told her that he thought the physiotherapy was not going to be enough.

"It's more of a general time frame. I should have a date confirmed in a month or so." She tipped her head. "Did you decide if you're going into the library or not?"

Will chuckled. "Yeah, I can wait for Eddie."

"I have coffee at my house," she said as she started rolling towards the library. "And I did not eat all the cookies I made, nor have I given them all away." She stopped and looked at Will. "I even have oatmeal chocolate chip – not a raisin to be found in that batch."

"Are you inviting me to your house for coffee and cookies?"

"That's exactly what I am doing."

"But you just got here."

She nodded. "And I was here before as well. I'm just stopping by to see how Lacey did with her interview."

"You knew about that?"

Her wheelchair stopped again. This time, she turned it towards him. "How did you know about it?"

Oh. He swallowed. Mistake number three for the afternoon. "Lacey told me."

"Did she?" There was a calculating glint to his grandmother's eye.

"Yes, and do you know what else?"

She shook her head as she said, "no."

"You might be right." He started walking toward the library. There was no way she was not going to follow him, and both the movement and the change of subject might get her off the topic of how he knew about Lacey's interview.

"Of course, I'm right, but what am I right about this time?"

Will laughed outright at that. "About my needing to consider hiring someone."

"Oh dear."

He stopped. "What? What is it, Gran?" He looked her up and down, but she appeared to be alright.

"You have come to that conclusion already?"

Was that the problem? Why would she be upset that he had finally agreed with her? "Yes, I have, and I thought you'd be happy about that."

"Well, if I had known you were going to come to your senses so quickly, I wouldn't have given Lacey that application for the library so soon." She huffed and shook her head as if disgusted with herself.

The pieces were falling into place. "Wait. You want me to hire Lacey?"

His grandmother shrugged and her head bobbed as if she really didn't want to admit what he said was true. "Didn't you open the resume I sent you?"

"No, I filed it in the *look into later* tab in my email since it was not urgent."

She blew out a breath. "It's Lacey's resume."

"Does she know you sent it to me?"

Again, she shrugged, and her head did that *I don't want to tell you yes, but I have to* bobbing and weaving thing. "She guessed it from what she heard of your conversation with me."

"And she's ok with you sending her resume to people?"

His grandmother grimaced. "That's why I was baking cookies."

Ah, apology sweets. His grandmother was known for those.

"And do you have any with you today?" he asked.

"I gave them to Edmund to give to her."

"Is she angry with you?"

"No, not at all. She was a little embarrassed, but at least, this time when I mentioned the idea of working with you, she was not opposed to it like she was the first time I mentioned it."

Will pushed the wheelchair button to open the library doors. "You discussed her working with me before?"

"When she said she was looking for a job."

He trotted through the door after his grandmother who had suddenly started moving faster. It was almost as if she was running away from this conversation. If she could take the stairs and not the elevator, she might have escaped, but she couldn't take the stairs.

"Why did she think working for me would be a bad thing?"

"Does it matter to you what she thinks?" She smiled slyly as she backed herself into the elevator.

"I'm curious. That's all." The lie made his ears burn. Hopefully, his gran wouldn't notice.

"If you say so," she said as the doors slid closed in front of them, and Will pushed the floor button.

"Why didn't she think she could work for me?"

"It was a look. That's all I know. Sometime during your first meeting, you looked at her sister critically."

That was it? One look and he was written off? Or *had been* written off – she seemed to have moved past that now, but still – one look?

"Oh," his gran added, "there is also that thing about you not thinking well of a literary great."

He closed his eyes and groaned. Jane Austen was going to be the death of him. He just knew it.

"I was talking to Edmund earlier," Gran continued, "and he mentioned they just got a couple more DVDs of Austen adaptations processed. If you're lucky, you might find one or two still on the shelf."

"Why would I want to borrow one of those?"

She shrugged. "Because you're not just curious, and..." She lifted her cane to emphasize her point. "You knew Lacey had an interview today."

"I don't see how those things mean I need to watch actors prance around in coattails and long dresses while reciting lines from a two-hundred-year-old book."

"Oh, look! Lacey is still here and talking to Edmund – who, you know, likes Jane Austen and is just as handsome as you."

"Gran."

She jabbed the button to open the door with her cane. "Don't Gran me, William Bennett. You like her, and I know it. Now, if you want me to *not* share that information with anyone – especially your mother – you'll borrow one Austen movie and watch it – before Sunday." She gave him a pointed look and wheeled her way into the library toward Lacey.

CHAPTER 10

—❦—

"And you're all set." Edmund slid a new library card across the counter to Lacey.

"Thanks, I appreciate it." The bar code on her old library card was nearly worn completely off. The numbers were still there, which enabled her to borrow things online, but it would not work in person at the check-out machines.

"It's what I'm here for."

Edmund's words registered faintly in her mind as her eyes caught sight of his older brother and her heart seemed to skip a beat. He certainly was handsome and, since she had decided that he was not a jerk but was, instead, a guy she'd like to date, the pull she felt towards him was becoming irresistible. She had even doodled his name in her journal last night.

"It looks like you're the main draw to the library today," Trish, another one of the librarians, teased Edmund.

"I'd say it's not me, and it's Lacey since Gran has been here twice today. However, Will is here, so it can't just be Lacey." He gave Lacey a look that added a *can it?* to his statement.

"It's definitely you," she said with as light a laugh as she could muster. Had she been too open in her admiration of his older brother? She would have to work on that if they were going to keep their whatever-it-was between them a secret.

"I don't care who the draw is," Trish whispered, "as long as whichever one of you it is keeps the yummy treats like your grandmother's cookies and brother coming." She sighed. "You Bennett brothers. Mmm, mmm, mmm. Deliciously handsome." She sighed again and shook her head as she wandered off to do whatever she had to do.

Edmund laughed as she left.

Lacey did not. Instead, she forced a smile to cover her unease. Didn't it bother him that Trish had ogled his brother and then inferred that all the Bennett brothers were yummy treats? It bothered Lacey because it felt far too familiar.

"Did it go well?" Barb asked.

"It did," Lacey answered. "I don't want to get my hopes up just yet, but I came out of there with a good feeling."

"They'd be foolish not to hire you," Barb said. "And

I am saying that as someone who has seen your resume." She grimaced. "And who will not send it to anyone else without your permission."

"Thank you." She peeked at Will.

He shrugged. "I haven't even looked at it. I just filed it in the *look at later* folder. Maybe if your name had been in the subject line, I would have looked at it, but it wasn't there."

"Am I missing something?" Edmund asked.

"Gran sent me Lacey's resume because she thinks I need office help."

"You do," Edmund said at the same time Barb did.

Will chuckled. "I'm beginning to believe it."

"Yeah?" Edmund's voice was filled with curiosity. "What happened?"

Lacey was curious about that, too, since the last time she had heard him talk about needing help with Barb, he hadn't been very receptive to the idea.

"Why do you think anything happened?"

Even Lacey could tell that Will was hedging with that question, and she hadn't known him very long.

"Because the big brother I know never admits to needing help until forced to do so." Edmund folded his arms across his chest and glared at Will.

"I missed a couple of kind of important things," Will said with a shrug that Lacey was sure was a cover for how much missing any details bothered him. He did not strike her as someone who overlooked anything of importance – at least, he did not overlook things on purpose.

"Will is coming to my house for coffee and cookies," Barb inserted. "And I have enough for everyone."

Will shot his grandmother a less than pleased look. "Actually, I was coming here to see if you wanted to go get coffee, Edmund, and Gran intercepted me."

"You're not turning down my cookies, are you?" Barb's look for her grandson was withering.

"No, I am not, but I did want the facts to be known."

"All the facts?" Barb smiled and fluttered her lashes.

Will's eyes closed. "No, just the ones about the coffee." His eyes opened again.

Were Will and his grandmother always like this? Lacey nervously tapped her new library card against her phone and hoped that their argument did not blow up into something more than a few pointed comments.

"So, coffee at my apartment?" Barb asked.

"Sounds good to me," Edmund answered.

"And you?" Barb's attention turned to Lacey, who wasn't sure she wanted to spend time with Will and his grandmother at the same time if they were going to argue. She also didn't want to disappoint Barb.

"It will have to be up to Cari." That seemed the

easiest way to shirk her responsibility and not succumb to her immediate urge to flee a disagreement. She hated the way she still did that. Why did it have to be so hard to overcome anxiety?

"If you give me her number, I'll ask her." Barb rummaged through her purse and pulled out her phone.

Lacey held out her hand. "I'll put her number in there for you." There really didn't seem to be another option. What Barb wanted, Barb got. Or so it seemed.

"Gran said you get off in half an hour," Will said.

"Yep. I just have a few more things to finish up," Edmund answered. "Did you want a computer today, Gran?"

"Of course."

"Then, let me sign you up for one." He pulled out his phone and tapped on the screen just like he had the other day when Lacey and Barb had been here. "Number six is available, and there's plenty of room at that table for your chair."

"I can get out of this thing and sit in a normal chair," she retorted.

"I know you can, but time is not on your side if you want us to have coffee when I get off work." He stepped out from behind the desk. "I'll make sure you're settled. It's on my way to the back room anyway." He turned to Lacey. "I hope you'll be able to join us for coffee."

Just over his shoulder, Will was scowling. Did he not want to have her go to his grandmother's house for coffee?

"Thank you," she said to Edmund.

He and Barb began to move toward the computer room, but partway there, Barb stopped and held up her phone.

"You're coming," she said.

"Gran," Edmund scolded. "Inside voices only."

Lacey chuckled at the way he reminded her of the teachers at the elementary school where she had worked for a while last school year.

"Hi." Will had come to stand beside her. "I need help."

She blinked. "You haven't even looked at my resume."

He shook his head. "I meant with picking a movie."

"Oh." Well, that was embarrassing, a fact her cheeks were all too willing to display.

"I've only just begun thinking about hiring help," he added quickly, which only made her embarrassment deepen.

"What movies do we have to choose from?" It was best if they moved away from the topic of Will and her resume.

"I don't know. I haven't looked yet."

Her brow furrowed.

"I have to pick one from here," Will added.

"You *have to*?" That did little to clear Lacey's confusion.

"Walk with me to the movies?"

She nodded and fell into step with him.

"I messed up," he whispered.

"How so?"

"I let Gran know that I knew about your interview. Sorry."

The movies were shelved close to the front desk, and they were now standing between two bookshelves. The one in front of them was lined with hundreds of DVDs, while the one behind them housed books.

"She is threatening to tell my mother that I like you if I don't borrow a Jane Austen movie and watch it before Sunday." He exhaled as if he had been asked to do the most horrendous task. "I don't know which one to choose."

"You like me?" she asked softly.

He nodded. "Is that ok?"

"I find it excessively agreeable," she replied while stepping sideways to where the few Austen adaptations that remained on the shelves were.

He followed her. "I think that's the first time I have ever liked something being said in an Austen fashion."

"There is a lot to like about Austen."

His sour look told her that he did not believe her. At. All.

"I will admit that period dramas can be dull for some, but..." She tipped her head and studied him. She was almost certain he could find some entertainment in a period drama if it was the right sort. After all, long dresses, tailcoats, and carriages did not guarantee she would like a film. Her tastes were not so easily defined, and she doubted that his were either.

"Did you do well in school?" she asked.

"Yes."

"In literature class?"

"Yes, but not because I enjoyed dissecting stories."

She smiled. It was as she had suspected. They likely had some similar tastes. That was good to know.

"I didn't like that part either," she whispered. "And the stories that we had to read were, for the most part, *not* ones I would have chosen."

"Exactly!"

Lacey pulled the 2005 *Pride and Prejudice* film from the shelf. "I'm surprised they have a copy of this." She turned it over in her hands. The last time she had tried to reserve it, which was about a year ago now, the waiting list had been so long that she had given up and purchased a digital copy instead of placing a hold. "It looks brand new."

"Gran said they just got some new ones of these sorts of movies."

"That explains this movie being here and looking so good." She held it out to him. "This is a personal favourite. There are other versions of *Pride and Prejudice*, but this one will likely suit you the best."

"It doesn't look like the one my mother watches," he said as he took the DVD case from her. "Hers is in a box, and the cover is not as interesting as this one."

"She probably has the miniseries." She leaned towards him. "It's six hours long."

"Six hours!"

"Shhh." She couldn't help giggling at his horror. "The miniseries is six hours, not that one." She pointed at the one he held, and his whole body sighed in relief.

"You said that this is one of your favourites?"

"Yep. The purist will say it does not follow the book as closely as it should, but I disagree. This one better captures what I feel is the essence of the story. However, I have a soft spot for symbolism and unspoken storytelling in films."

He turned the case over in his hands. "I have to admit I'm slightly intrigued." He looked at the case he held. "How am I going to get out of here without Edmund seeing what I'm checking out and wondering about it?"

"Use the self-scan while he's in the back?"

"But that would mean leaving now."

She nodded.

"And I don't want to." His eyes held hers, and he took a step closer to her, leaving only an inch or two of air between them. "I wish I could invite you over to my place to watch this with me, but that would mean involving others to keep rumours about impropriety from circulating in church. I'd like to know what you like about this movie. It might help me enjoy it more."

And she would love to see and hear his reactions to the movie as they happen. "I own a copy of that one, and I have a phone." She wouldn't be able to see his reactions this way, but she would be able to hear them in real-time rather than waiting until he could tell her how he liked it at some point in the future.

His lips tipped up on one side. "Are you suggesting we watch separately while on the phone?"

"I am, but we can use an online message app if you prefer. Staying on the phone for over two hours might be a bit much." And ten-finger typing was faster than two-thumb typing.

His smile filled itself in. "I find I'm actually looking forward to watching this now."

"There you are. What movie are you getting?"

Will's eyes grew wide with horror as Edmund

entered the aisle they stood in. He held up the DVD in his hand.

"*Pride and Prejudice?*" There was no lack of shock in Edmund's voice.

"I was just telling him about one of my favourite movies," Lacey said, taking the DVD from Will. "I was happy to see a copy here, and I have that new library card. The borrowing period for this is a week, right?"

"Not that one," Edmund replied. "That's pretty popular, so it's only three days." He came around to her other side. "You know, this one is better." He pulled out the miniseries.

Lacey shot Will a questioning look.

"Edmund is an Austen fan." Will said it as if it was a fault.

"Oh, how interesting. I haven't met too many guys who are."

"He also loved literature class," Will added, as if that was a greater flaw.

Lacey's eyes grew wide with understanding. Edmund was what she was not – a Jane Austen purist.

"I suppose that makes sense with the English degree he said he has," she said.

Hopefully, he didn't have any say in whether or not she got hired, because she was not going to check out a box of DVDs that she knew Will would struggle to get through. She didn't mind the miniseries, but when given the choice between it and the one she held... "I think I'll stick with this one."

"Are you sure?" Edmund asked as if he couldn't believe she would choose the movie she held over the box he held.

"Positive. I find this one does a better job of portraying the essence of what I read in the novel."

His eyebrows flew towards his hairline. "Oh... well... ok."

Lacey smiled at his stammered politeness. "It is fine if you disagree with me so long as you do not disparage me for my choice."

He chuckled. "I can agree to that."

Lacey pulled another DVD from the shelf.

"Don't tell me you also prefer that version of Emma?" Edmund's tone was slightly condescending.

"Do you have the one with Johnny Lee Miller?"

"No."

"Then, I will settle for my second favourite." She clasped both movies to her chest. "I think I'll sit outside and wait for Cari. Do you want to join me?" she asked Will. "It would be less boring if I had some company, but I completely get it if you'd rather hang out inside." She tried to keep her tone nonchalant so that it sounded as if she was just asking a friend, and not a guy that set her heart fluttering, to sit with her.

"Sure. I can sit with you."

"Well, then, I suppose I'll go check out." She slid past Will and was just exiting the aisle when she heard Edmund.

"You two were looking awfully cozy."

"We were looking at movies."

It sounded as if Will was following her for his voice did not grow softer as she walked toward the check-out station near the front desk.

"Is there anything you want to tell me?" Edmund asked.

"Nope. Not a thing. Don't you have work to do?"

Edmund chuckled. "I do, but you're infinitely more interesting."

Keeping this whatever-it-was between her and Will a secret was going to be anything but easy. Could she call it a relationship? They were probably going to have two phone movie dates. One was confirmed. The other was just a hope.

"She's pretty."

Edmund was obviously digging for information.

"Not blind." Will's retort was sharp, causing her heart to flutter and not in a good way. "See you at Gran's," he said as he joined her at the checkout.

She looked over her shoulder. Edmund was smirking as he returned to his position behind the front desk.

"Brothers," Will muttered in the same disturbed tone he had used with his grandmother earlier.

"Frustrated?" she asked as she took the slip that told her when to return the movies from the check-out machine.

"Yes. Sorry."

"Do you always get snappy when frustrated?" she asked.

"I try not to, but yes, often." His face squinched up as if admitting that was painful.

They stepped out of the library, and he took a deep breath.

"Snappy makes you nervous, doesn't it?"

She looked at him in surprise. "How do you know that?"

"I'm pretty sure I've never exited the library as fast as we did just now."

"Sorry." She settled onto the top step and turned her face to the sun for a moment. "I wish it didn't make me nervous and want to run away, but it does."

"Is there a reason why?" He asked as he sat down next to her.

She nodded and pointed at the two-inch white gash on her upper arm. "My father. I got between him and mom when he was angry."

She shook her head, not wanting to remember being tossed aside into the table with the vase that broke and cut her. Nor did she want to remember how he had yelled at her for being so clumsy and how he had yanked her to her feet and smacked her while her mother shouted at him that she was bleeding. That night, after the ER visit, she, her mother, and Cari had left and never returned.

"I own this *Emma* movie, too, and it doesn't have to be returned for a week." She handed both movies to him. "You should stash these in your truck before anyone joins us."

He did not move. He just kept looking at her. "I would never..." he finally said.

"I don't want to talk about it," she whispered. "Maybe someday, but not today."

He nodded. "Just know that, with me, you are safe. Always."

He took the movies from her and went to his truck while she looked at the clouds above her and willed herself not to cry at the sweetness of his words.

CHAPTER 11

Will wasn't sure who was the most nervous about today – he had not slept well, Emma had called him twice yesterday before Cari and Lacey arrived at her apartment, and Lacey had texted him multiple times to ask about how and when they would present the no college idea to Will's parents.

"I'm going to have to put sidewalk repairs on the next budget proposal," his dad said as he came out of the church and joined Will on the front walkway. "Is there a particular reason you are out here pacing?"

"I'm just waiting for Emma."

"And her friends?"

Will nodded. "I want you and Mother to like them." And not just for Emma's sake.

"We will."

Will wished he could believe that. His mother was not going to be happy to hear that Emma was not going to college.

"Hey," Edmund called as he got out of his car. "Are we forming a receiving line?"

"No, Will is just waiting for Emma and her friends."

"Is he?" Edmund smirked at Will.

"Yes." Younger brothers could be such an annoyance. "I said I would meet Emma here when she called me yesterday." He had also told Lacey that when she had texted before going to sleep. However, he was not going to share that bit of info with Edmund because Edmund did not need another reason to tease Will about Lacey. Friday's movie picking at the library had been enough to fuel that.

"What are we all waiting for?" Henry asked as he and his two good friends, Tyler and Blake, joined them.

Henry and his friends had been meeting for Sunday morning pre-church breakfast for years. In fact, it was that pre-church breakfast that had helped Blake come to Christ. Henry was a tease of the first order – much worse than Edmund – and rarely serious for long, but that did not mean he did not take his faith seriously. When Henry was sold out to something, he was all in, and his faith was one of those things.

"Emma, Cari, and Lacey," Edmund replied.

"Who are Cari and Lacey?" Henry asked.

"Emma's friends," Will answered before Edmund, who was still smirking, could. "And possibly Blake's and Tyler's new neighbours. Well, Cari will be in a few weeks, and Lacey might be for a while if she gets that job at the library."

"I'm pretty sure she's got it from what I heard on Saturday," Edmund said.

"You worked on Saturday?" That was unusual for Edmund.

"Only for two hours. With Jenna out having her baby and it being summer vacation time, we were shorthanded during the *Moms and Tots* time, and I could use the overtime pay."

"Don't tell me they let you entertain the children," Henry said with a laugh.

Edmund shook his head. "Nope, I filled in on the front desk."

"There's Emma's car," Mr. Bennett said. "We should probably go inside and let Will greet Emma's friends alone so that we don't overwhelm them."

"I'll go meet them at Emma's car." Will wasn't going to risk having one of his brothers pushing the issue and trying to stay with him – and by one of his brothers, he meant Edmund. He had seen how Edmund had admired Lacey at the library and at Gran's on Friday. He wasn't sure if the admiration at Gran's was real or just something Edmund was using to torment him, but he really did not want to give his baby brother a chance to commandeer Lacey's attention this morning.

As it turned out, it wasn't a brother about whom Will needed to be concerned. Nate had pulled his motorcycle into the parking lot just behind Emma.

"Today's the big day, eh?" Nate asked as he tucked his gloves into his helmet and stashed it in the bike's trunk.

"Sure is." Cari tugged at her top.

"Nervous?" he teased.

"Excessively," Emma said.

"Aw, you'll be fine." Nate tossed one arm around Emma's shoulders and the other around Cari's. "If not, just call me and I'll rescue you. I'm going to be at Mom's today."

"Hi, Will," Emma said. "Thanks for being here to meet us."

"What are big brothers for?"

"Tormenting," Nate said. "At least, that's what I've heard from my business partner."

Emma laughed and so did Cari.

"Everyone ready for this?" Will asked as he finally allowed his eyes to move to Lacey. It had been torture to not look for her first, but he knew he had to play the part of big brother, and not boyfriend, at the moment. That word still made him smile just as it had on Friday when Lacey had given him permission to think of himself as her boyfriend and for him to consider her his girlfriend.

"I think we are," Lacey answered. Her hands were tightly clasped in front of her, and he so badly wanted to take one of them in his own. However, he couldn't.

"Tyler and Blake are here, so I can introduce them to you."

"Why are you introducing them to those two?" Nate asked.

"They're going to be my new neighbors," Cari answered, "and Lacey is a good big sister who worries far too much about her little sister's ability to be around single guys."

"Is she worried about me?" Nate whispered.

"Are you single?" Cari asked.

"Yep."

"Then, that's your answer."

Lacey huffed.

"What are big sisters for?" Will said with a laugh. "Although it should be noted that worrying about little sisters is not the sole domain of older sisters. Older brothers also worry." He tipped his head toward the church. "It will be less awkward if we get to Sunday school class before it begins."

Lacey nodded and her shoulders lifted and lowered noticeably.

"Hey," Will said as they started walking, "it's going to be ok." At least, he hoped so.

She smiled at him, and suddenly, he felt as if what he had said was true. That wonderful, hopeful feeling stayed with him right up until they reached the doors of the church.

"Lacey, Cari, this is my brother Henry and his friends, Tyler and Blake."

"Henry, that's me." Henry patted his chest and grinned broadly. "Tyler," he pointed to his right. "And Blake." He pointed to his left. "I'm happy to meet any friends of Emma's."

"It's nice to meet you as well," Lacey said while Cari stared down Blake.

"Do you two know each other?" Henry asked. Apparently, he had noticed Cari's stare as well.

"Yeah, but not by name," Blake replied.

"Well, not proper names, at least," Cari added. "Steal anyone's parking spot today?"

"Didn't steal one today or yesterday, Princess," Blake retorted.

"I clearly had my turn signal on."

"Couldn't see it from the direction I was coming."

"I was slowing down to turn into that spot."

"I thought you were slowing down to let me go ahead of you. You know, because I thought you were a courteous driver." He made a scoffing sound. "Clearly, I was wrong."

Lacey stepped between Blake and her sister. "I say let bygones be bygones." She gave Cari an angry glare. "Especially at church," she hissed. "Please," she added in a whisper.

Cari shrugged as if she wasn't willing to let the matter drop.

"The parking spots at the apartment are assigned and numbered, right?" she asked Will.

"Yes, they are."

"Good. Then, we shouldn't have a problem, as long as he parks in his spot and not mine."

"Welcome, welcome!"

Will had never been more thankful for his father's friendly manner than he was at that moment, for it meant that Blake did not have a chance to retort. Will knew that would make Blake seethe for a while. However, it would also let Cari have the last word and, therefore, would make Lacey less nervous.

"You must be Lacey," Will's dad extended his hand to her. "And Cari," he shook her hand after Lacey's. "We are delighted to have you join us today. I understand you will be moving to Hatfield Falls, Cari. I hope you'll make our church your home."

"I'd like that," Cari said with a smile.

"And if you get that job, Lacey, we would, of course, wish the same for you."

"Thank you, Pastor Bennett. I hope that wish comes true."

"My wife was just checking on the cookie supply in the toddler nursery and instructed me that she wanted to meet you before Sunday school so that she would be able to concentrate on the lesson instead of anxiously waiting to meet Emma's friends." He motioned to the open doors of the church.

Lacey's shoulders did that lifting and lowering things again, and without thinking, Will put his hand in the middle of her upper back to guide her as he whispered, "It will be ok."

Henry cleared his throat, catching Will's attention. When Will looked at him, he only smirked and cocked an eyebrow before looking at Will's hand.

Will snatched his hand away from Lacey's back. "I'll be right with you," he said, then he dropped back to where Henry was.

"She's nervous about meeting Mother."

"That's a good excuse."

"It's the truth," Will snapped and then closed his eyes and grimaced. "Can we do this later? I really don't want to add to her anxiety with our arguing." He kept his tone cool and level.

Henry's eyes grew wide, and he blinked. He was

probably surprised that Will did not rise to his bait as expected. "Sure," he said.

"And don't tease me about it in front of Mother. I was just trying to be a good friend." Which was true. Though there was more to it than that.

"Sure. If that's what you want." Henry's words were accompanied by a teasing smile. "How long have you known *Emma's* friends? Because you seem to know one of them quite well."

Will blew out a breath. "Later or I will tell Mother how you really got that sprained ankle last month."

Henry nodded. "Right. Later."

Will knew that trying to sneak into someone's second-floor apartment through the balcony door was not on the mother-approved reasons for how an ankle was injured. And so did Henry. It wouldn't matter to their mother that the sneaking in was just to play a prank on a friend's brother.

He sighed when he turned back toward the church. Edmund had joined his father and Emma and was standing next to Lacey. He gave Will a taunting look when he saw him.

"I'm sure you don't have anything on Eddie, so good luck with that." Henry slapped Will on the back as he passed him.

"Do you?" Will called after Henry.

His brother snorted. "Are you kidding? No."

"Brothers, eh?" Tyler said. He was the brother who had been pranked in the sprained ankle incident. "They can be royal pains at times."

"You know it," Will agreed.

"Seriously," Tyler said quietly. "She seems nice. Good luck. And don't worry about me saying anything. I won't."

"Thanks, man." It was the closest Will had gotten to a confession that he and Lacey were more than just friends.

"I'd be happy to run interference if you need it," he added before giving a nod and then, trotting down the hall to catch up with his brother and Henry.

Lacey looked in Will's direction just as he saw his mother crossing the foyer. He took four long strides and reached the group just as his mother did. "You, ok?" he whispered.

She nodded.

"Emma, we don't have much time," his mom said, "but I simply must meet your friends before Sunday School, or I am absolutely going to perish from curiosity."

Introductions were made. His mother cooed her pleasure in meeting them. Then, his father indicated it was time to move along to classrooms.

"You'll go with Emma, of course," his mother said to Cari and Lacey. "I'm sure either Will or Edmund would be happy to sit with you and make sure you have everything you need."

"Will can," Emma blurted. "He already promised," she added hastily when everyone looked at her. "I mean, Edmund can join us, of course. There are always rows of empty seats. I'm sure we'll all fit."

A twinkle of something shone in his mother's eye. It was a something he was certain he wasn't going to like. "Ah, yes, Will should join you. He is the eldest." She motioned for him to lead the group to the singles classroom down the hall.

"So I have heard," Edmund muttered.

"So have I," Will commiserated. As much as his younger brother disliked being told he was younger and, therefore, less qualified due to simple birth order, Will also disliked that it was always assumed that he was the one to lead, to have the answers, to know the way, to be right, to never fail.

"Come on," he said. "Let's try to not be the last ones in the room. Maybe we can sit with Henry." Not that he really wanted to, but saying so probably made it seem less like he wanted to keep Lacey to himself – even if that was exactly what he wanted to do.

CHAPTER 12

—⁓—

Lacey pushed open the swinging door that divided the front entry of the Bennett's home from the kitchen. So far, the day had gone well. She had survived all the introductions to people at church whom she would likely only remember by face and not name. There had been so many! She supposed that was not due only to her and Cari being new to the church but also being attached to one of the pastor's kids.

"Can I help you with anything?" she asked Mrs. Bennett. The woman was a virtual hummingbird, flitting from one thing to another.

"That is kind," she replied. "But there is not much to do." She stopped in the middle of the expansive kitchen, right where an island might be in any other house, and whispered, "I have a system."

"For everything," Henry said as he passed through the propped-open swinging door from the dining room to the kitchen.

169

"When you have six children, you'll know why," his mother retorted.

"I'm not going to have six children."

"One never knows these things. The number of children you have is up to the Lord." She held up a hand as Henry opened his mouth. "We have guests. Save your shocking comments for when we do not, or better yet, just forget them altogether."

She lifted the lid on one of the three crockpots on the long counter that ran the length of the wall from the dining room door to the window on the back of the house.

"Has Brandon set the table?"

"Yes," Henry replied. "That's why I'm getting the water from the fridge."

"And Gran? Has her chair been parked?"

"On the porch."

"Where is Will?"

"Talking to Dad." Henry stopped at the door to the dining room. "Do you have any other questions before I pour water?"

"No." She bent and pulled a serving platter out from a lower cupboard. "For the roast," she explained to Lacey.

"Can I hold it while you lift the roast out?"

Mrs. Bennett chuckled. "Are you feeling useless?"

"A trifle."

She froze with two forks poked into each end of the roast in the crockpot and her elbows bent upward like a flapping bird and turned her attention to Lacey. "I don't hear that word very often." There was a hopeful look in her eye.

"I use it a lot because I think it sounds better than *a bit* or *a little* and is more descriptive."

"I wouldn't disagree with that. I also like it because it harkens to a time gone by." Mrs. Bennett returned to her work of lifting the roast out of the pot and placing it on the platter. "Just put that platter over by the sink," she instructed.

Then, she tore open a gravy packet and whisked the contents into the drippings from the roast. "My mother despises that I use this." She lifted the packet. "But she never had five boys to feed and keep from killing one another while cooking." She laughed.

"How did you do it?" Lacey was truly curious how anyone could survive having so many children underfoot, for from what she had been told, the boys' ages were all close together. And she had also noted that they all seemed to hold their mother in high regard, even if they did tease her and seemed to fear her to some extent.

"I prayed. A lot! And I came up with systems to keep them busy." She poked her head out of the door that went to the front entry which was attached to the living room.

"William. Five minutes," she called. Then, she returned to whisk the gravy once more before dipping the tip of her pinky into it and tasting. "Delicious," she declared.

"Do you have Sunday dinner here together each week?"

"As often as possible." She sighed. "I dread the weeks when we aren't able to gather. It is far too quiet."

"I imagine it was never quiet when your children were all growing up."

"It was when it was just Will and Brandon, but then, once Henry arrived..." She shook her head. "Your mother was wise to stop at two," she said with a laugh. "Although I wouldn't give up even one of them, they were a challenge. Emma was a piece of cake compared to her brothers. Even when she became a teen."

Mrs. Bennett bustled around the kitchen gathering bowls and serving spoons while she spoke.

"I dreaded the teen years because I had heard and seen a few horror stories, but Emma has always been the most obliging child."

Until now, Lacy thought as she said, "That must have been a blessing."

"Oh, it was. If only the boys had been so easy." She took the lid off the second crockpot. "How were you and your sister as teens?"

Lacey picked up the bowl next to Mrs. Bennett and held it while she put potatoes in it.

"There are no horror stories, but I can't say we were always obliging. We had our moments of willfulness, but neither of us ever rebelled. Mom had a hard enough life without either of us adding to it."

Once again, Mrs. Bennett froze mid-task. "I hope you don't mind, but my husband told me some about your father. He thought I should know." She returned to her task.

"I don't mind. It's my history and not a secret. However, it's not something I find easy to discuss."

She shot Lacey a sympathetic look. "I can imagine it's not." She placed the last potato in the bowl. "I also imagine it's not something one forgets or that does not cloud the way things are viewed."

"You would be right," Lacey admitted.

Mrs. Bennett removed the lid from the final crockpot that was filled with carrots, turnips, and cabbage.

"In this house, and with my boys," she said, "you and your sister are safe. Not one of them has a disagreeable temper. Not that they do not argue and fight. They have even been known to hit each other and end up wrestling, but they know how to treat a lady. Mark and I made certain of that."

"From what I have seen, it appears you have done a good job."

"They are all single," she said before beginning to scoop vegetables into a bowl. "And that is all I am allowed to say on that. Apparently, my matchmaking is not welcomed." She laughed. "Not that I do it because it is welcomed. A mother's children sometimes need a little push to move in the right direction."

"I suppose they do," Lacey muttered just as Will entered the kitchen, followed by Frederick.

Frederick took the bowl of potatoes to the dining room while Will pulled out an electric knife.

"People still use those?" Lacey asked, crossing to the counter by the sink where Will was beginning to carve the roast into slices.

"I don't know if anyone else does, but Mother insists upon it."

"It does the best job," Mrs. Bennett inserted.

"It certainly appears to," Lacey agreed. "Mom would have liked one of those."

"Would you like to give it a try?" Will asked.

"No, I'd be afraid to ruin your work. I don't think I've ever seen a roast beef sliced so evenly."

"Will is meticulous," Mrs. Bennett said. "Of course,

he has also been in charge of carving the Sunday roast ever since he was ten."

Lacey blinked. "He carved it every Sunday for – how many years it that?"

"For twenty years."

Wow. That was a lot of roast cutting.

"He has gotten better over the years. You should have seen the first few." Again, she laughed. Laughter seemed to be ever-present in the Bennett house. It was so different from her own rather quiet home.

"I was ten," Will protested.

"No one was criticizing," his mother assured him before going to the dining room to deliver the gravy boat to the table.

"Do you struggle with perfectionism, too?" Lacey asked. She had started attempting to be perfect to avoid her father's displeasure and punishments as a young child and had never really given up the practice.

"I do. I wish I didn't, but I do."

"I know the feeling. I wish I could break that habit, but it's well-ingrained."

"I don't think I've ever tried to break the habit." He looked at her with a hint of surprise. "I just always thought it was part of who I was."

"Perhaps it is, but that doesn't mean it has to rule a person. Or so I've been told."

"Yeah?" He removed the blades from the knife, rinsed them, and put them in the dishwasher. "Who told you?"

"Pastor Anderson. He's been helping me work through some things related to my dad."

Will leaned against the counter.

"He keeps reminding me that the only one who is perfect is God, and I'm not supposed to try to take His place." She shrugged. "It's that whole balancing trying to be what God wants me to be and not allowing it to become the ruler in place of God that's the hard part."

"Makes sense," Will said.

"The meat, Will." Mrs. Bennett was at the door to the dining room. "I'm going to call everyone to the table."

Will took up the platter. "Come on. You don't want to get trampled by the herd of hungry Bennetts."

"I doubt they would trample anyone."

"Likely not," Will agreed. "At least, not now. However, when we were younger, we did race to see who could be the first to sit down."

Lacey laughed as she imagined five little boys pushing and shoving each other to get a chair first as if it was a game of musical chairs.

"I have you and Will on either side of Gran," Mrs. Bennett said to Lacey as the others joined them.

Barb entered the dining room, walking with only a

small limp and with Edmund's assistance, and Lacey waited until Barb had taken her seat before she took her place.

"How was the movie?" Barb whispered to Will.

"Not as dreadful as I thought it might be," he replied.

Will had been an excellent student of film during their online date on Friday night. That being said, he had also been extremely happy that the movie had only been a little over two hours long while at the same time, he had been disappointed when their chat both about the movie and life had drawn to a conclusion an hour after the movie had ended. Lacey had to admit it was the best date she had ever been on in her life.

"Then, I am keeping my knowledge to myself?" Barb glanced from Will to Lacey.

"Please," Lacey replied.

Barb's eyes lit with delight. "Do the feelings go both ways?" she whispered.

"Telling secrets at the table is not allowed," Henry said.

Lacey could see why his arrival in the Bennett family had shaken things up. His wit was as quick as his motions, and he did seem to be always moving – much like his mother.

"I'm an eighty-one-year-old woman with a bad

hip," Barb grumbled. "I can whisper to my friend if I want to." She shot a questioning look at Lacey but thankfully, did not repeat her question in words.

Lacey gave her a slight nod.

"Excellent." She then pretended to lock her lips just as Pastor Bennett indicated that it was time to pray.

~*~

"You don't mind that your grandmother knows, do you?" Lacey asked later when she and Will were outside with Emma, Cari, and Thor.

"She already knew," he replied.

"Surviving?" Nate called across the fence.

"Yep, so far," Will replied.

"So, I can't come eat cookies with you?"

"I'll send some over to you and your mom. Will that do?"

"I suppose it will have to."

"I suppose you're right," Will replied. "How's your mom today?"

"She thinks she'll be strong enough to tolerate people next Sunday."

Lacey watched Will and Nate talk and wondered what was wrong with Nate's mother.

"His mom just finished chemo," Emma explained as she and Cari joined Lacey and Will at the fence.

"Did it work?" Lacey asked.

"They think so, but there are tests to be run later."

Lacey wrapped her arms around her middle. "That has to be hard for him." Having an ill parent was challenging. Losing that parent to a disease was even harder. She hoped that Nate did not have to experience that last part.

Emma nodded. "Yeah, it has been for all of us, but not as much as it has been for Nate." She shifted from one foot to another. "I want to get this secret keeping over with," she whispered.

"I asked Dad to get Mother out here before tea," Will said as he threw the ball once again for Thor since his conversation with Nate had ended and his friend was headed back to his house. "There's no need to involve the others."

"What don't the others need to be involved in?" Brandon asked.

There seemed to always be someone or another around. How did anyone keep anything a secret in this family? Lacey had found it challenging enough to keep her date a secret with only one sister in their house.

"I'm not going to Bible college," Emma said.

"Good. What are you doing instead?"

"Taking some cooking classes and opening a café."

Brandon bent down and scratched Thor's ear. "Hey, buddy," he said to the dog who was seated at his feet. He glanced up at Emma. "If you need pictures done, let me know." He scratched Thor's ear again. "Come on, Thor. Let's go find Gran." He looked at Emma again. "If you need more than pictures, you know my number."

"That's it? No other questions?" Will asked in surprise.

Brandon shook his head. "If this is what Emma thinks she should be doing, then she needs to do it. Attempting to fit into a mould just because it is expected is dumb. Trust me. I know."

"Amen!" Cari said before giving Lacey a look that said, "*See?*"

"What?" Lacey said. "I never said you had to fit into a mould."

"True. You never *said* it."

"There is not fitting into a mould and then there is trying to spite the mould with drastic decisions."

Brandon held up his hands. "Sorry. Didn't mean to start something. However, since it appears I have, I'll add that sometimes drastic decisions are necessary."

"Are you ok?" Emma asked him.

"Yeah, sure. I'm fine. I've just spent a week and a half alone in a tent, so I've been thinking." He smiled at his sister. "I'm sure I'll be back to normal in a few days." He clucked to Thor, and the pair headed back toward the house, just as Pastor and Mrs. Bennett exited it.

"Taking Thor to Gran," Brandon said as he passed them. His father patted him on the shoulder as if it was some sort of congratulations on a job well done.

"Tea is almost ready," Mrs. Bennett said, "but your father said there was something you wanted to talk to me about?" She cast a hopeful glance between Will and Lacey.

"I'm not going to Bible college," Emma blurted. Apparently, she had not been kidding about wanting to get this over with. "Cari and I are going to start a café – well, a food truck, and then, a café – and we're taking cooking courses at the community college. I've already enrolled."

Mrs. Bennett's mouth dropped open.

"Their business plan looks good," Will inserted. His voice was calm and exuded confidence. No one would ever know that he was nervous about how his mother would take this news and his involvement in it. Lacey only knew because he had mentioned it on Friday.

Will's mother's eyes shifted from Emma to him.

"But... Bible college..." Her tone was one of disappointment.

"I know you want me to find a good husband," Emma said, "but I can do that without Bible college."

Mrs. Bennett's eyes grew wide. "Is that why you thought I wanted you to go to Bible college?"

"It's the first reason you give whenever you talk about it," Emma answered.

Her mother shook her head. "I wanted you to go to Bible college for the atmosphere and education. Where better to dip your toes into the adult world and make good friends and solidify your faith?" She shook her head again. "I'm not sure I can support this idea."

"I can," Pastor Bennett said.

His wife spun towards him. "You can?"

He nodded. "Emma is not foolhardy."

"But..." she cast a look in Cari's direction.

"Mrs. Bennett," Lacey inserted as her stomach tumbled. She truly had no desire to enter into this argument at all, but she also couldn't just stand by and allow her sister to be thought of as a bad influence, which is what she suspected Mrs. Bennett was currently thinking. "I didn't think this was a good idea to start with either."

"You didn't?" Will asked.

"No," she looked up into his surprised eyes and held his gaze. "I wanted my sister to find a more conventional path to her future."

"How so?"

"I wanted her to return to college and finish her

business courses before finding a stable job and setting up her own home."

"But –" Cari attempted to break into the conversation.

"But..." Lacey shot a look at her sister before turning her attention to Will's mother, "I listened to Cari on her way to meet with Will and Emma on Monday, and I've been pondering that conversation and coming to terms with things since then."

"Let's sit by the firepit," Pastor Bennett suggested. "And then, perhaps Lacey can share what has changed her mind."

"We can sit, but I'd rather let my sister share with you what she shared with me." They – most especially Mrs. Bennett – needed to see the determination in Cari's eyes and the excitement that always overtook her when she spoke about this venture.

And Cari did not disappoint. She oozed conviction when she spoke about how she had prayed for someone like Emma to be her business partner, and joy radiated from her when she began talking about the possibilities that lay before her and Emma.

Mrs. Bennett sat quietly for some time after Cari finished speaking. Then, she shook her head and said, "I'm still not sure. It seems risky."

"It is," Will said. "But they will have me to help them. They are not going into this alone."

"And I know that Lacey will help us when and where she can," Cari inserted with a glance in Emma's direction.

"Will you?" Emma asked Lacey.

"Of course, I will, although I am not sure what sort of help I can be other than to be an encouragement for you."

"Encouragement is important," Pastor Bennett said.

"Do you really think this is a good idea?" Mrs. Bennett asked him.

He took her hand. "Emma seems to have found two very good friends who will help her grow in her faith. She also has our church and inter-church activities for that. You know she's always been an excellent cook and baker because you encouraged her to pursue that interest from the moment you recognized it. And as she's said, she and Cari will have Will and Lacey to help them." He smiled. "I'm sure she'll have the support of all her brothers and your mother, as well as many others once this plan is shared with them. But none of that really matters. The only question that must be answered is if Emma thinks that God is calling her to this, who are we to stand in her way?"

Mrs. Bennett sighed. "When you put it like that, the only thing I can do is agree, but I still have some reservations."

"Reservations are natural," her husband assured her.

"We were thinking that maybe we could cater some church singles events," Cari inserted. "It would be a great place to demonstrate your daughter's accomplishments."

"*We* were not thinking that! You were." Emma crossed her arms and glared at Cari.

Mrs. Bennett's lips tipped up in a tentative smile. "That could be a good idea."

"Who knows," Cari said with a grin, "maybe an apple pie might catch her a Mr. Knightley."

Emma smacked Cari's arm.

"A Mr. Knightley?" Mrs. Bennett said with some interest. "Do you like Jane Austen?"

"I don't complain too overly much when my sister subjects me to it." And that was about as much as Cari liked all things Austen. They were tolerable but not interesting enough to tempt her into true devotion.

"Well, then," Mrs. Bennett said, sounding a great deal more optimistic than she had since the discussion had started, "perhaps this could work."

"The tea is getting cold," Henry called from the back door. "And Frederick is threatening to eat all the cookies."

"Tell him he'd better not!" Mrs. Bennett was on her feet and headed toward the house.

Pastor Bennett gave Henry a thumbs up.

Lacey shook her head. She had never considered that a pastor could be scheming, but apparently, there was, at least, one who was. It made him seem more like a normal person to her.

"So, that didn't go as poorly as you thought, now did it?" he asked them.

"No, not at all," Emma answered.

"And he told me only God worked miracles," Will muttered as he rose along with the rest of them to follow his mother into the house.

"What?" Lacey asked.

"Nothing," he replied. "It was just something Dad said when I visited with him about this earlier on Tuesday." He shook his head and then smiled. "I guess bringing our plan to my father was a good idea."

"So it would seem," Lacey agreed. "Do you think you can return that movie for me? It's due tomorrow."

He nodded and then, did that same thing he had done this morning. He put his hand on her back and gave her a gentle nudge forward, and just like this morning, his touch was gone too soon.

CHAPTER 13

Will looked up from his laptop when the door to his office squeaked open. He should likely fix that squeak, but it was handy in a doorbell sort of fashion. No one could sneak in. It was like that step that his father refused to fix until after Will and his brothers had all moved out. The brother most likely to have needed that sneaking in or out alarm of a squeaky step was the one who had just entered Will's office.

"I've got a lead on a possible bus," Henry said as he let the door close loudly behind him and headed to the fridge.

"Why do you want a bus?"

Henry pulled one of those coffee beverages that Lacey liked out the fridge and popped the top. "It's not for me, genius." He dropped onto a sofa and tossed his feet on the table. "These are my clean shoes," he said before Will could complain about him getting the table dirty.

Tapping his manager's name badge, he added, "I'm on my way to work."

"My office is nowhere near to being on your way to work."

"Today it was." He chugged half of his drink. "The bus is for Emma and Cari. A fella who stopped in at the automotive department yesterday said he had an old bus his wife had wanted him to convert into a tiny house on wheels, but before he could do more than rip out the interior, she left him for some guy with a yacht. Anyway, he's looking to get rid of the reminder of his ex – although he used much more colourful and derogatory terms for her. I think he'd be motivated to take a reasonable offer on it just to get rid of it."

Henry pulled a card out of his shirt pocket. "He wrote his name and number on the back of one of our service appointments cards. If you're interested, you can give him a call." He placed that card on the table. "Take Fred with you. He's not on the schedule again for three days."

Frederick not only shared a house with Henry and Edmund, he also worked as a mechanic at the department store Henry managed.

Will pushed his chair away from his desk and rose. He could use a break from the numbers and a cup of proper coffee. In the two weeks since Emma had revealed her plan to their parents, he had been scouring the internet looking for a vehicle to create into a food truck. He hadn't considered a bus. Leave it to Henry to think outside the square truck box.

"Is this guy local?"

"He lives halfway between here and Marydale. Just past the convenience store with the big ice cream cone sign."

That was promising. Will dropped a pod into the coffee machine. "I'll give him a call this afternoon." Right after he called Fred and checked on good times to go view the bus. "Do you know anyone with a bus license who can drive it back here for us?" Neither Cari nor Emma had a license beyond the normal car license.

"Check with Blake."

"Blake?" The guy who oversaw delis for a grocery store chain? Why would he have a bus license?

Henry nodded. "I think he's got certification that would cover a bus."

"Why?"

Henry shrugged. "Why not? He used to do some deliveries for the store before he started working with the delis. I think he still fills in on a route or two when he can for the extra cash."

Will guessed that made sense.

"Now, tell me what's up with you and Lacey."

Henry looked at his phone. "I've got half an hour, and you just started drinking your coffee."

"What do you mean? Lacey and I are helping Emma and Cari get things set up for their business."

"Eddie says you've visited the library more in the last week than you ever have, except maybe when you had a paper due back in high school."

Well, that was true, and he had to admit that visiting the library to see Lacey was far more enjoyable than going there to research and write. But did he want to tell Henry that? Not really.

"There's a lot to do to get a food establishment up and running." He kept his eyes on his coffee. Henry was too good at reading people. It was best not to make eye contact.

"Nope. Not buying it." Henry's feet came off the table, and he leaned forward. "I never teased you about how friendly you were with her at church the first Sunday she visited, so spill it. I've decided I don't care if Mom knows I hurt my ankle climbing into Tyler and Blake's place."

Will cocked a skeptical brow.

"Seriously. I don't care."

"Why would I tell you *if* there was anything to tell?"

"Because I can keep secrets."

That was true. Telling a secret to Henry was like

locking it away in a safety deposit box. It was rare that he shared them.

"Here's how I see it. You like her, and you don't want Mom to know until after you have managed to ask her out on a date and found out if she likes you. Right?" He folded his arms and leaned back, obviously satisfied with himself. "If it helps any, Eddie thinks she likes you, and Gran seems to agree – or so Eddie says."

Will shook his head. "I already know that she likes me." Would it really hurt to let Henry in on the situation? "You will not share that fact with anyone – not Mom, not Eddie, not Gran, not Blake or Tyler, no one."

Henry held up his hands as if trying to ward off Will's glare. "If you tell me everything, I'll even promise not to tease you about it. Unless we're alone," he added after a half-second's pause. "Come on," he said when Will didn't answer immediately. "You and I have shared lots of secrets over the years."

That was true. Henry was the brother Will had been most likely to confide in. Brandon was too philosophical about things at times, and if he told Fredrick or Eddie anything it was like telling them both.

"Ok." He blew out a breath. "We're dating. *Secretly*." He emphasized the last word. "We haven't told anyone. Gran knows because it was the only way to keep her quiet about the possibility of my liking Lacey." He chuckled. "She made me watch an Austen movie as payment for her silence."

Henry laughed. "You watched an Austen movie?"

Will nodded. "I've watched two actually."

"Two? Gran made you watch two?"

"No, she only required one. Lacey gave me the other one and offered to watch them both with me." He shrugged. "It wasn't too awful. I mean I did get to hang out with Lacey."

Henry's head was shaking slowly. "This is the problem with women. They make us guys do dumb stuff and like it."

Will laughed. "Watching movies is not doing dumb stuff."

Henry snorted. "It is when it's a girl's movie."

"I'll have you know that they were both adaptations of books that are taught to girls and boys alike in some high schools. So, I'm not going to classify them as girl's movies." The rom-com he and Lacey had watched last night was most certainly a girl's movie in his mind, but he wasn't going to offer that info to Henry. However, he was beginning to understand his father's answer about love making you do things you never thought you would whenever he was asked why he had allowed their mother to name them after literary characters.

"Do you love her?"

"I don't know." That was a question Will had found himself wrestling with recently. "We've only been secretly dating for a couple of weeks. I think it might be too early to call it love." Even if that is exactly what it felt like.

"Dad would disagree."

"Yeah, I know. He fell in love with Mom after one date."

The room sat silent for a moment while Will drank his coffee, and Henry watched him. Just when Will was about to tell Henry to stop staring, his brother asked another question that hit at the heart of Will's thoughts regarding Lacey, and one he was equally not ready to answer.

"Have you thought about marriage?"

"Doesn't everyone when they start dating someone?" Will hedged. "It would be silly to date someone without having thought about if you could see yourself marrying that person."

"You know what I mean."

He did, but that didn't mean he wanted to answer the question.

"Well?" Henry asked.

"Well, what?"

"Have you thought about marrying Lacey? And not

just in a *would she be a good possible wife candidate* sort of way but in a *I'd like her to be my wife* sort of way."

Will blew out a breath. "Yes. Which is ridiculous. I know what Dad has said, but I don't do things like that. I plan. I draw up schedules and charts. I plot things out. I don't jump into things." Not that his father was not a planner. He was. He planned out lots of things for the church and its ministries. But that was different – or, at least, Will was unwilling to allow it to be the same. Normal people did not fall in love in two weeks. Did they?

"Ah." Henry nodded his head as if he was a wise old sage who understood everything. "And that is why you don't want Mom to know about this relationship; because Mom can make a great system when needed, but she's not known to hold back and contemplate when it comes to romance."

Will nodded. Maybe Henry was a wise old sage. "You know that she'd have us married off in a month."

"A month? By next Sunday is more like it," Henry said with a laugh.

"True." Their mother was eager to have one of her children get married. They all knew it, as did everyone in the church. It was hard to hide when she asked for prayer that she would become a mother-in-law soon.

"And is Lacey ok with keeping things a secret?"

Will's brow furrowed. She seemed to be. "I never

asked, but she never pushed against the idea either. It seems she has a sister who is hoping to marry her off." Still, it was something he might want to clarify with Lacey.

"I'm glad Emma isn't like that. Can you imagine both Emma and Mom working together to marry us all off?"

Both Will and Henry laughed at the thought as the door to the office squeaked open once again.

"Hey," Lacey said as she stepped inside. "I told Emma I would drop these cinnamon buns off for you and Nate before I went to work."

"Were you at Emma's?" Will asked. She hadn't mentioned joining Cari when she got together with Emma today.

"No, she was at my house. She and Cari are working on recipes while filling out their business plan." She placed a container on the counter near the fridge. "Any coffee left?"

Will lifted his cup. "Lots."

"Not that kind. The good stuff," she replied with a laugh.

"Don't know. Go ahead." He nodded to the fridge.

"You like those, too?" Henry asked as she popped open a cold-brewed coffee.

"They're a weakness."

Will motioned to the chair next to him. "Do you have some time before you have to be at the library?"

She sat down. Apparently, she did have time.

"So what are you guys up to?"

"I was on my way to work and wanted to let Will know about a lead on a bus that can be made into a food truck," Henry replied.

"Cool." She sounded genuinely delighted with the news. The longer the idea of her sister being a food truck owner sat with Lacey, the more accepting of the idea she seemed to become.

"And then, we were sharing secrets." Will gave her a pointed look.

"Oh, that sounds fun?" she asked with a wary glance towards Henry.

"I'm better than Gran at keeping secrets," Henry said. "And I'm happy for you." He stood. "Do you need me to stay as a chaperone? I'll assume if you've been on secret dates that you don't need one."

"Those have been over the internet," Will said.

"How do you date over the internet?"

"Chat apps and movie streaming services," Lacey answered.

"Are those the only dates you've been on?" It was surprising that neither of Henry's eyes fell out of his head and went rolling across the floor with how wide he had opened them.

"No, we've met for coffee twice and gone on one walk in the park in Marydale," Will said.

Henry shook his head. "You guys need to improve your repertoire. Dinner, a real in-person movie, things like that. Something less like casual friends."

"Without Mom knowing?" Will asked.

Henry's features pinched into a pained expression. "True. It would be harder to keep things secret, and on that note, I will add that you might want to be a bit more careful at the library if you don't want Eddie knowing more than he thinks he already does."

"Would it hurt to tell him?" Lacey asked.

"Not if you don't mind Fred and Brandon knowing, and possibly Emma and, I will assume, your sister," Henry replied.

Lacey sighed. "And that would make it harder to keep from your mom."

Will nodded.

"I'll leave you to sort that out," Henry said. "Behave," he added with a wink before ducking out the door.

Lacey sipped her coffee drink silently after the door had closed.

"Are you ok?" Will asked.

She nodded. "I'm just wondering why you don't want your mom to know about us. I like her, and I kind of hate keeping this a secret from her."

"Do you want Cari to know about us?"

She shrugged. "At first, I didn't. But now, I'm not sure why I didn't." She smiled at him. "I wouldn't mind telling all the world that you're my boyfriend."

He followed her to the kitchenette where she rinsed and disposed of her drink container and Henry's. He would have to speak to his brother about cleaning up after himself later.

"And I'd love to tell the world you are my girlfriend, but you don't know what my mom is like with these things. There would be albums of baby photos to go through, mentions of possible names for future grandchildren, hints about rings and dresses and how lovely weddings in December can be, and on and on and on." He shook his head. "And it wouldn't be confined to just our family. The whole church would be involved."

He knew intimately how bad it could be. He had been through this once before when he had foolishly thought to invite the girl who he had just started dating to a church activity. It had been their second and final date. That had been back in high school. He and his brothers had been branded as the boys with the nutty mom and getting dates to do more than meet at school events or in groups at fast food places or movie theatres had become a challenge for a while.

His mom had apologized for her exuberance, and,

to her credit, she had been somewhat reserved when Brandon had brought home Zoe, whom he had been dating fairly seriously. Their mom had not been the demise of that relationship, but Will was still not certain his mother wouldn't be too enthusiastic if she knew he was dating.

"It's nice being just us without an audience of several hundred." In a large family, and being that it was a pastor's family, there was little which was ever just his to know and enjoy.

He took her hands when she turned toward him. "I'd like to keep it a secret for just a while longer. Maybe until the food truck is up and running and we're both really sure that this – us – is what we want – what God wants. However, if you would rather tell everyone now, we will."

Her eyes held his for a long silent minute. There was some uncertainty in them. "Just for a little while?"

He nodded. Was he doing the right thing asking her to let him have some time where she was just his alone?

"Until we know that we want *us* in a forever kind of way?"

Again, he nodded. It was best if they had some time to consider where they were headed before the chaos of his mother and all the ladies at the church entered into things.

Lacey expelled a breath.

"I know I'm asking a lot of you, but it will get noisy once everyone knows," he added. "It might be easier to decide the future without that noise."

"I suppose you're right."

It was not a ringing endorsement of his plan, but it would have to do.

He tugged her closer to him. "I like you more than I have liked anyone ever, Lacey."

She smiled. "That goes both ways."

"Really?"

She nodded. "No guy has ever watched *Pride and Prejudice* and *Emma* for me or with me."

He laughed. "Is that all I've got going for me? A willingness to watch period dramas?"

Her brow furrowed and her lips pursed in a most adorable teasing expression. "No, you're also not a jerk."

His eyes grew wide. Had she thought he was a jerk at some point? "I'm happy to hear that."

"And kinda cute."

That was better. "Kinda?"

"Yep." Her eyes were dancing with amusement. "Which is way better than just tolerable, Mr. Bennett."

He chuckled and then, shook his head at the fact that he found a reference to *Pride and Prejudice* amusing instead of annoying. "I guess I should be happy that a lady as tempting as you finds me to be more than tolerable."

"Ok, now we're both being silly," she said with a laugh.

"I wasn't kidding." He released her hands and framed her face with his hands. "You are loveliness personified."

"Oh." It was more of a breath than a word.

"You won't slap me if I kiss you, will you?" He leaned his head closer to her lips.

"I might if you don't."

That was all the permission Will needed to close the gap between them and taste her lips. They were heavenly with a hint of mocha. Perhaps he could learn to like those bottled coffees, he thought, as her arms wrapped around his waist and her lips willingly parted to allow him to deepen the kiss.

"Alrighty then. I'll just wait outside for a few minutes."

Nate's voice startled Will. He hadn't even heard the door squeak.

Slowly, reluctantly, he stopped kissing Lacey.

"How is Nate with secrets?" Lacey asked him when he stood there holding her and letting his heart rate return to normal.

"Not as good as Henry, but not as bad as Edmund."

"You know keeping this a secret is not going to be easy after that kiss," she said to his chest, which is where her head rested against him.

"Not at all," he agreed. "Because I'm going to want more of those."

"Me, too."

"Is it safe?" Nate called from the door.

"Yeah," Will answered. "I need to talk to you." He gave Lacey one more quick kiss before releasing his grip on her.

"You sure do," Nate said.

"Have a good day at work," Will said to Lacey, ignoring his friend for now.

"Are you stopping by later?" she asked.

"I don't think I should." Even if he wanted to.

"But you'll call me later?"

"You know it." And he'd likely text her a couple of times before that.

"Good." She stepped away from him. "Hey, Nate. Emma sent cinnamon buns. I was just dropping them off before work." Her cheeks were a pretty shade of pink.

She stopped at the door and turned back to look at Will and wave.

"Do I get to eat all the cinnamon buns if I pretend that I never saw what I saw?" Nate asked.

Will picked up the container and looked inside.

"Nope. I get one, but you can have the other three if it will help your memory fade."

Nate took the cinnamon buns from Will. "So, you and Lacey, eh?"

"Yep, me and Lacey." Were there three more wonderful words? A smile tipped his lips on one side. He was pretty sure there weren't. "But no one knows except for you, Henry, and Gran." That list kept growing.

Nate sank his teeth into a cinnamon bun. "You sure keeping it that way isn't worth four cinnamon buns to you?" he asked around the bite he was chewing.

"Nate," Will growled.

His friend laughed. "Ok, ok. You can't blame a guy for trying. So, three cinnamon buns and details. All the details." He motioned to his desk. "Come along, Mr. Bennett, we have matters to discuss."

Will shook his head at the high falsetto voice Nate used but followed him to his desk and took a seat, where he shared the extent of his and Lacey's blossoming relationship with his best friend.

CHAPTER 14

"Where's Eddie?"

Lacey jumped and dropped the book she was about to shelve.

"Sorry," Will whispered as he took a place leaning against the shelving unit. "I didn't mean to startle you. I'm just hoping to avoid seeing my brother today, but I couldn't stay away from you."

Ever since Henry had cautioned them two weeks ago about being too obvious about their relationship around Edmund, Will had begun sneaking into the library to see her, and not his brother, for a few minutes each day, and, while, at first, it had been fun and made her feel special, she had to admit that it was starting to annoy her.

"I couldn't think of a good reason to give him for why I'm here," Will added.

"You could always tell him the truth."

Will's brows furrowed and his gaze became intense

as it always did when he grew serious about something. "I can if you want me to."

Oh, she wanted him to, but she also didn't want him to. That was the most frustrating part of all of this. She wanted him to not care if his mother acted like a crazy hopeful mother-in-law. She wanted him to joyfully proclaim that she was the one he had been waiting all his life to meet.

However, she also did not want to put him in a place that would make him feel uneasy and would add stress to his life – especially now that he had run into a few snags with his housing project. His and Nate's time schedule had been utterly obliterated by a permit that still needed to be acquired from the city. The same one that she had called Doreen about dropping off to them all those weeks ago.

She took her time slipping the book she had retrieved from the floor into its proper place on the shelf. Will was not good with sudden schedule changes. She had learned that he struggled just as much, if not more so, than she did with putting things in God's hands and leaving them there. They had chatted at length about it during their online "dates." She had shared her fear of not being able to protect her sister, and he had touched on his fear of failure. She longed for the day when they could sit in the same room and discuss things like that. That day would come. It just wasn't going to be today.

Deciding that her desire to see him well overshadowed her desire to date openly, she shook her head. What girl wanted to push her boyfriend into acknowledging her publicly? Not Lacey. Besides, they only had to keep up this charade until the food truck – er, bus – was ready to roll, and Cari had said last night that it should be ready for inspection in two weeks.

He caught one of her hands before she could turn back to the shelving cart.

"You only have to let me know."

"I know," she assured him. "The last I heard, Edmund was working in the acquisitions room, so we're safe."

He squeezed her hand.

"What have you been up to today?" she asked as brightly as she could.

"Several things. I met with a potential real estate agent I might be able to use for my flipping projects and even the new builds, and I just checked on the kitchen and bathroom at Cari's place before coming here. She should be able to move in next week as planned without having to live in much of a construction zone. We're just waiting on the flooring for the guest bedroom. I plan to give your sister a call later to let her know."

Lacey pulled her hand away from him and picked another book from the shelving cart. As much as she'd love to stand here and hold his hand, she was at work, and not even holding Will Bennett's hand was going to keep her from doing her job. She had overheard a conversation the other day about a possible permanent position opening up soon, and she wanted to make sure she was in a good position to put her name forward as a candidate for the job.

"Have you decided what to do about your place?" Will asked.

"No, I haven't. I keep vacillating about what is best. However, you will be pleased to know that Cari has persuaded me that driving forty-five minutes each day to work – especially in the winter – is not ideal." She placed the book she held in its home on the shelf and then, pushed the cart down one set of shelves to where she knew the next set of books belonged. "I know a lot of people drive that far or further for work, but..."

She turned toward him. "Their whole after-work life, or a good part of it, tends to be where they live, and Cari will be here and you're here, and I'd like to go to church with you and her." She shrugged. She loved the comfort of her mom's house, but she knew that it was soon going to be a lonely place to live.

"Renting it out instead of selling would give you

the option to go back if you decided to, and it would provide an extra source of income."

She had heard that suggestion from both her sister and him before. "It will also provide a source of concern when things go wrong and need fixing. I'm not a handyman, Will."

He smiled softly at her. It was such a caring expression. "Talk to Nate. See what kind of arrangement you could work out with him about handyman services. He has more resources than I do since I tend to rely on his crews to do a lot of my work, and I've heard him offer that sort of service to some of the elderly people at church."

That would make the idea of keeping her mom's house and renting it less frightening.

"Would you help me find a tenant and work through the leasing process and all that?"

"Absolutely. I'd be happy to help you with anything."

And she loved that about him. That word – love – was one she found herself using more and more often when she thought about Will.

He pushed off the bookshelf. "I suppose I shouldn't keep you from your work, although I'd like to," he added in a whisper as he stepped closer to her. He leaned towards her, but the buzz of his phone stopped him from closing the distance and kissing her.

"Bad news?" she asked when she heard his sigh at whatever was on his screen.

"It might be. Or it could be good." He typed his reply. "At least, now, I have a reason for being in the vicinity of the library."

"City stuff?"

He nodded. "Someone wants to talk to me about that permit."

"So, you still haven't gotten it." Last night, he had been hopeful that the permit would be in today's mail. Apparently, it hadn't been.

"Nope. This guy went on vacation early and came back with ideas about what he thinks I should do with my project and is holding my permits hostage until I hear him out."

"Can he do that?"

Will shrugged. "Seems he is." He leaned toward her again, and she met him halfway for a quick kiss. "You know if you worked for me, I could kiss you better than that without you getting into trouble." He held her face between his hands, seemingly unwilling to let go of her too soon.

She laughed. "And I still think that dating my boss is not a good idea. Besides, you aren't truly ready to hire someone."

"I could be."

"But you're not."

He kissed her once more, this time in a lingering, longing-filled fashion. It was the kind of kiss that made a girl's legs go wobbly and urged her to forget about possibly being discovered, just so she could kiss him for longer and feel his arms around her body.

"I could be," he whispered before he took a step back from her. "I'll let you know how the meeting goes." He wiggled his phone as he moved down the row of books toward the open library area, indicating that he would call or text and not reappear at the library.

She stood there, allowing all the wonderful feelings that kissing him always brought to wash over her. He stopped at the end of the aisle and peeked around the last bookcase to see if the coast was clear before heading toward the door.

"Well, that was interesting."

Lacey jumped and her hand flew to her heart.

"I believe, Miss Lacey Welsh, that I just saw Will Bennett kiss you and say he was going to call you later. Here I thought we were becoming friends, and you're holding out on me."

"Hey, Trish. I'm just about done with this load of books."

"Mm-hmm, I can see that, but that's not what I want to know about." She took a book from the shelving cart. "Spill it. I've been wondering why that beautiful man has been hanging around the library so much. I know he has said it had to do with your sister, but I thought there might be more to it than that." She held up the book she had taken from the cart. "Tell me what's up with you two, or the book gets misshelved."

Lacey laughed. "You wouldn't purposefully misshelve a book."

Trish opened the book and flipped through the pages. "I'm not sure if I care about this book getting lost. Gardening is not my thing."

"But it is the thing for many of our patrons."

Trish sighed. "I'm just not tough enough for the godfather life. However, I have one sister and two brothers, so I am not too soft for the 'I'll tattle on you' life. In fact, I'm shockingly good at it."

Lacey did not doubt that since Trish was the second eldest child in her family and only a year younger than Lacey.

"I'm thinking Edmund might be interested in knowing what I saw, and I'm also thinking that from the way Will was playing spy trying to avoid detection just now, you two don't want Edmund to know about that kiss."

Lacey had to give it to Trish. She definitely knew which panic buttons to press.

"Ok, you got me there, but you cannot tell anyone about that kiss. Or Will and me."

Delight danced in Trish's eyes. "Ooooh, so there is a Will and you? I'll shelve these; you talk." She snatched the book Lacey was holding from her hands.

Lacey swallowed, looked up and down the aisle, and then, leaning forward, said, "We're secretly dating and have been for about a month." The words rushed out of her in one breath.

"Oh, honey!" Trish cried in a loud whisper before lowering her volume again. "I would not be hiding that I was dating someone as yummy as Will Bennett."

"You might if he asked you to."

Trish turned toward Lacey with her mouth hanging open. "He asked you to not tell anyone?"

Lacey nodded.

"Does he have another girlfriend somewhere?"

"No."

Trish arched one of her perfectly contoured eyebrows at Lacey. "He wouldn't tell you if he did. But I hear a lady sometimes knows these things without being told."

"He's not hiding our dating from another woman unless you count his mother as the other woman."

"Why would he hide you from his mother? She seems like a nice lady, and she's a pastor's wife." Trish folded her arms. "In fact, now that I think about it, why is a pastor's kid asking you to be sneaky? Seems to me that pastor's kids ought to know better than to be sneaking around kissing secret girlfriends in the library."

Lacey knew that Trish had a bit of a hang-up about churches and all things religious, and she did not want Trish to be able to add this to her arsenal of complaints about those things.

"I don't know what it's like to be a pastor's kid," she said, "but I would imagine it can't be much different than being any other kid, except, perhaps, that there are more people watching you. We all have things we don't want to tell our moms sometimes, don't we?" Although, honestly, Lacey was struggling to think of anything of great importance she had ever hidden from her mother.

Trish pondered that for a moment. "Ok, I can see your point. Will Bennett is not a saint, just a pastor's kid. But that does not answer why he would hide dating a pretty thing like you from his mother."

Lacey shrugged. "To be perfectly honest, I don't get it completely, but he insists that his mom will go over-the-top excited if she knew, and he'd like to keep it private for now instead of publishing it to the whole church."

Trish shoved the book she held into place and then leaned toward Lacey. "Lots of moms are that way. Mine would be a good example. She started picking out names for grandkids when my older brother mentioned he was dating. I don't know why that would be an issue."

Lacey blew out a breath. "I don't either, but it is. So..." She shrugged.

"And you have lost your heart and mind to him." Trish smiled wistfully. "I hear love makes people do crazy stuff."

"It seems to be true," Lacey said with an uneasy laugh. "Not that I'm saying I love him."

Trish's expression changed to disbelief. "Oh, honey, you love him. I might not have ever been in love before, but I know what it looks like. I've had enough friends leave me for a guy to know the look, and you've got it." She sighed. "Can we still be friends until you get married?"

Lacey's brow furrowed at the odd question. "Yes, but I don't see why we can't be friends after I get married as well."

Trish laughed. "You just admitted you have thought about marrying him."

"I did not." Although it was true that she had considered it. Often. Daily.

"Oh, you did, and to answer why we can only be friends until you get married, that's when I have lost all my other friends. I did get to be a bridesmaid and dance with some pretty good-looking groomsmen as a parting gift, though."

There was a hint of bitterness in Trish's tone that tugged at Lacey's heart. She had heard that same tone in her sister's voice whenever she talked about the no-good-loser who had dumped her.

"I'm sorry."

Trish brushed her words away with a shake of her head. "It's just how life goes. They moved up a level, and I'm still here, hoping to someday find *the one*."

"Hey, give me a chance. I might not be like your other friends."

Trish gave her an appraising look. "Well, you've managed to get Will Bennett to date you, and from what Edmund has told me, that puts you in a class all by yourself. I guess I can give you a chance, but just so you know, I won't be surprised if married life just pulls you away. Most of the others didn't mean for it to happen either. It really is just how life goes."

"Well, it shouldn't be," Lacey said with no little amount of conviction, and she'd work hard to make sure it wasn't. Trish claimed to be a Christian even though she refused to go to church or church events. Someone, somewhere, had hurt her badly, and Lacey would not let herself add to that.

"I like you, even if you do frown at me when I tell Edmund how much I appreciate his good looks."

Lacey's eyes grew wide. She hadn't thought Trish had noticed that. "Sorry, I don't mean to frown. Truly

I don't, but I had a boss who used to say those sorts of things to me before he started to let his hands wander. It's kind of just a reflex I suppose."

It was Trish's turn to sport surprised eyes, though her eyes likely looked bigger than Lacey's did due to Trish's exceptionally long lashes – the result of a terrific mascara that was expertly applied.

"Oh, I feel dreadful." Trish groaned. "I post all the time on social media about how horrible sexual harassment is." She blew out a quick breath as if she had been punched in the stomach. "But... Edmund doesn't seem to mind." She groaned again. "Yeah, that sounded lame."

"Maybe he doesn't. I don't know what your relationship is like. I'm just the new girl, coming into the library with all my baggage."

"No, no, you have a point. I should stop. But he really is cute."

"He is." Lacey looked behind her to make sure the aisle they stood in was empty and then whispered, "but not as cute as his brother."

Trish laughed. "I'll let you think so."

"You won't tell anyone about Will and me, will you?"

Again, Trish gave Lacey an appraising look before saying, "Nah. I won't tell."

Lacey breathed a sigh of relief.

"Friends have to have each other's backs, right?"

"Right," Lacey agreed.

"So," Trish said as she handed one of the last two books on the shelving cart to Lacey while keeping the other for herself, "is he a good kisser?"

"Oh, yeah," Lacey said as she crouched down to find where her book went. "He's make your knees weak good." And the only guy she ever wanted to kiss, secretly or otherwise, for the rest of her life.

CHAPTER 15

"Just think about it," Stan Tremblay handed the coveted permit to Will. "I would not have held up your getting this if I hadn't thought my ideas were of great value to you and the community. And I could not have explained this all to you in an email. I tried. I wrote and deleted three of them."

Stan, a gentleman of at least fifty, leaned back in his chair. "Your father is the pastor of Hatfield Falls Christian Church, right?"

"Yes."

"Then, am I free to speak about religious matters without it being offensive?"

Will eyed him skeptically. "I suppose so."

"Your application was on my desk before I left for my vacation. I don't know how I missed seeing it, but I did. I was unaware of my oversight until I was twenty-three hours into a three-day road trip to visit my in-laws. That's when Doreen called me and gave me the

219

once over for having left work undone." He chuckled. "She's great at her job and cares about the people she sees on the front line out there."

"She was willing to help me out in getting my application in on time."

"She and I go to the same church over in Wilson's Crossing, so she's more than just a co-worker. She's my wife's good friend. But that is neither here nor there really, other than to say that she encouraged me to tell you this." He grimaced. "I don't usually bring my beliefs into a conversation with someone seeking a permit. I try to make certain my beliefs and business practices match, of course, but otherwise, speaking about things of the Lord are left for during breaks and after work. We serve people of all backgrounds here."

"I understand." Will also was not one to insert God into all his conversations with workers and clients, but he did his best to make certain he was honouring God in all his business dealings. "God is present even if He is not named."

Stan smiled. "Exactly! Getting back to your application that went missing on my desk. Doreen told me what it was for, and I remembered seeing the article in the paper. As I have already said, I think what you're doing is wonderful. More businessmen need to be motivated by a love for people rather than a love for money. It's truly a great way to put our faith into action."

"Thank you," Will said as he started to feel a little less irritated about Stan's interference.

"Now, this part is perhaps going to sound a bit strange, but two days after Doreen called me, I had a dream about the plans I just shared with you, and I had it for three days in a row. The same dream. The same ideas. And when I signed and stamped that page yesterday and got it ready to put in the envelope, I felt this overwhelming sense that I needed to share my ideas with you before I gave that form to you." He nodded to the paper Will held. "I didn't grow up in a church that believes in dreams and premonitions." He shook his head as if completely baffled by what he had experienced. "I can't explain any of this, but I know that you needed to hear my ideas."

Will eyed the permit he held. Was God trying to get his attention through Stan? It wasn't impossible. It was odd but not impossible. "I will consider them."

"They could help you do more good – share more grace to those who need it, but I also understand that it would mean changing things for you. I suppose you already have things ordered and arranged."

"I did, but not getting the permit forced me to put those things on hold and cancel a few."

Some suppliers were more willing to work around

holdups than others were. The willing suppliers had been put on the shortlist for sources to contact with future projects, while the others were added to the "use only if necessary" list of suppliers.

"I truly am sorry about that, but nothing happens outside of God's timing, right?"

A smile tipped Will's lips. "A good friend has said that very thing to me." A sweet and kissable girlfriend, that is. Every time he grumbled to her about his schedule being ruined.

"Keep that friend," Stan said with a grin. "We all need people in our lives who will remind us of what's important." He stood. "Again, I apologize for not getting that paper to you before I went on vacation even if I do think there was a reason for it."

"I'm just glad to finally have it." Will also stood and held out his hand to Stan, who shook it. "Thank you, sir, for your time, your ideas, and your willingness to bring God into the room today. I will give what you said serious consideration."

"That's all I ask. It may not be what God wants from you. Your original idea might be His plan, but I had to share what I thought He wanted me to share."

Will thanked him again and ducked out of the office.

"Did you finally get it?" Doreen called to him as he crossed the main waiting room.

222

He held up his papers.

She shook her fists in the air like a sports fan cheering after their team had scored a point.

Will chuckled and pushed open the door. The wet and warm air of early August smacked him in the face, and he hurried to his truck and the air conditioning it would provide. He didn't mind warm weather, but when the air began to feel like a dripping wet sponge, like it so often did in August in Nova Scotia, he began to long for autumn.

He settled into his truck, and while the A/C began to do its job in cooling things down, he looked at the library, wanting with all that was in him to go back in there and tell Lacey about what Stan had said. However, he couldn't risk it. Two visits in one day would be suspicious to anyone, not just Edmund. So, instead, he pulled out his phone and typed *Got the permit*, adding a smiley-faced emoji at the end for emphasis.

Lacey wouldn't see the message until later.

Heading to the office. I'll call later. It was an interesting meeting.

He typed *love you*, then erased it and hit send. It would be best if those words were not first said in a text message. However, they seemed so natural to add to the end of his message that deleting them almost seemed wrong.

He put his truck into gear and made his way out of the parking lot and down the main road through Hatfield Falls. His phone, which was tucked into its holder on the dashboard buzzed.

"Answer," he commanded. "This is Will Bennett," he said when the phone connected him to whoever was calling.

"Will, there's a Tiffany Martin here to see you. Will you be back soon?" Nate said.

"I'm on my way there now. What does she need?" Tiffany was the realtor he had met with earlier today. He had thought they had covered everything about how they could work together on some projects.

"A tour of the place."

"Can't you give her a tour?"

"I tried that option."

Will pulled to a stop at the light on the corner of Main and Falls Road. "I'll be there in fifteen minutes."

"Can you make it any faster?" Nate whispered. "I don't like the way her aunt is looking at me."

Will laughed. "I bet I got that same look this morning."

"You saw Mrs. Martin and her niece this morning?"

"Yep. Tiffany is a realtor and new to town. Mom arranged for me to meet with them. I didn't want to. You know Mrs. Martin's reputation for meddling in the love lives of anyone who is not yet married."

"Oh, I do. I do. Can you drive faster?"

"I am not getting a ticket just to keep you safe from Mrs. Martin. However, I'll push it a bit, and you'll thank me by taking that tour with us."

"Deal."

"I got the permit," Will added before Nate could hang up. "We need to talk about the ideas Mr. Tremblay shared with me. They're good, but…"

"They're not yours," Nate finished.

"Yeah. That." Wow, that sounded arrogant. But his business was his business. He was the one who was responsible for making it succeed.

"Anything you can share about them now so I have a reason not to go over there and play host?" Nate's plea was bathed in desperation. Will couldn't fault him for it. He had wanted to leave his meeting this morning before it had even started due to the sharks-are-circling vibe Tiffany and her aunt exuded.

"What would it do to our timeline and returns if some or all of the lots became multi-family? The zoning is not an issue according to Stan."

"Multi-family? How many families?"

"Four minimum perhaps? And maybe three with a short-term rental as the fourth unit."

Nate blew out a breath, and Will imagined him drumming his fingers on his desk as he always did when pondering something.

225

"Did Mr. Tremblay give you any design ideas?" Nate asked.

"No. I was kind of hoping you might have some creative ways of stacking containers to make multi-unit structures. I can work on it once I get to my computer, of course. I don't mean to drop this on you."

"Will."

"Yes."

"Are we partners?"

"Yes."

"Then, we'll work on this together, or I'll do some designs, and then, you can calculate costs and revenue needed to make a good margin without gouging."

"Right. I just hate to dump this on you."

"Just trust me for once."

"I do trust you."

"Not as much as you trust you," Nate grumbled.

"I'm sorry."

"Yeah, I know. You always are. Are you almost here?"

"I can see the turn."

"Great. I'll let you go then."

"Oh, Nate, one more thing. When you're designing, can you try to include some off-grid things like solar or rainwater catchment for landscaping?"

"That will increase the price."

Will knew that, and so had Stan. "That's why the

idea is to be multi-unit with one investment unit to bring in higher income from business travellers and the like."

"Listen, we will discuss that later, but I'm thinking as a businessman on a trip, I would not want to be staying next to a family with loud kids or dogs or whatever."

That was an excellent point that neither he nor Stan had thought of. "Then, maybe we should think about a couple of four-unit rentals?"

"You are seriously considering this?" Nate's tone was one of shock.

"I am. I said I would, and so I am. I'm not saying I will go with this idea. I'm just doing what I promised and giving it careful consideration." And he'd be praying about it as well. There had been something that had tugged at his mind while listening to Stan's ideas, and it had felt a lot like what Gran called a God breeze.

"Ok, then. I'll see what I can come up with. I'll start on it now."

"See you in less than five. 'Bye."

The call clicked off, and Will sighed. "Tiffany." He shook his head. "Not going to happen, Mrs. Martin. Not going to happen."

He had known from the moment his mother mentioned the idea of his helping Tiffany get established in the Hatfield Falls real estate market that she and Mrs. Martin were playing matchmakers. However, no matter what they tried or who Tiffany was or what she was like, his heart was not available, for it was engaged elsewhere.

Tiffany had not appeared to be an unwilling participant in the matchmaking game. She had sat far closer to him than a professional should when they met for coffee. She said it was so her aunt could be close enough to hear. However, Mrs. Martin was not hard of hearing. She seemed quite able to catch the lowest whisper when it came to finding things out.

He parked his truck just as the door to the office opened, and Tiffany, in her black pencil skirt, ruffled pink shirt, and ridiculously high pumps, tottered her way down the metal steps, clutching the railing and taking care not to get her heels caught in the openings in the metal that let the rain run through the steps.

"Ms. Martin, Mrs. Martin," he greeted.

"Tiffany," Tiffany corrected. "If we are going to work together, you should really call me by my first name, Will."

"Oh, indeed," her aunt agreed. "We were taking a drive, and I insisted on stopping here. I thought it was a good thing for Tiffany to get an idea of what she might be selling for you."

"As you can see, there is not much to see. We have

cleared some lots, but nothing has been built." Will stood where he was but turned toward the road that led into the development as he decided that a tour was not needed. Tiffany would likely hurt herself if they tried to walk down the road to the first lot. "Five of the lots are on the water and the other seven are between here and there, and this one, where we are standing, will be the model home lot, which will double as my home and office."

"You plan to live here?" Mrs. Martin asked. "Does your mother know this?"

"No, I didn't think I needed to clear where I lived with her."

"Will it be a big place?" Mrs. Martin asked.

"Big enough for me and maybe a dog."

"Just big enough for one person?"

Will nodded. That was a little bit of a lie. Two people would fit snuggly into what he planned to build, and his plans could be changed for the right person. However, neither Mrs. Martin nor Tiffany was the right person.

"That might not be a good model home then," Tiffany said. "How is a family supposed to get an idea of space in something so small?"

"It's going to have to do." Will was not going to fall into their scheme to make him admit that the house he planned to build could be modified to accommodate Tiffany, because Tiffany was not going to be part of Will's future except for when it came to selling homes.

"It won't be long until we have an actual saleable unit ready," Nate said, joining the conversation.

"Are you going to live here, too?" Mrs. Martin asked.

"No, I have my own place in town, over on James."

"Is it nice?" Tiffany asked.

"Nice enough." Nate shot Will a look that begged for help.

"Did you see the ideas book in the office sitting area?" Will asked.

"We did. It's quite clever what can be recycled into something usable."

Tiffany did not seem as impressed with the housing units as Lacey and Cari had been.

"Well, God has told us to steward the earth," Will replied. He didn't care if she liked the houses or not. "Are you still interested in being invited to the realtors' open houses?"

"Oh, yes. I can sell anything. It can be a shack in need of major renovation, and I'll sell it."

"Then, as I said this morning, I'll make sure your name is there with the others."

"No special viewing for the niece of your mother's

friend?" There was a hint of disapproval in Mrs. Martin's voice.

"I am sorry, but that seems like it would be unethical, and Nate and I strive to keep everything above board."

Mrs. Martin smiled. "I told you that they were men of substance, Tiffany." She looked down the road. "How far is it to the lake?"

"Just over three kilometers."

"Are the roads passable?"

"Absolutely. Feel free to take a drive down to the water before you return to town. Of course, the view of the lake will get better once construction is further underway."

Mrs. Martin darted a look at Will's truck and raised an eyebrow.

"I'm sorry I cannot escort you down to the water. I have an important meeting with Nate about some plans. We're behind schedule, so it really cannot be put off." Nor did he want to be trapped inside the cab of his truck with Tiffany and her aunt.

"Oh, no, we didn't expect you to drive us down there," Tiffany said with a laugh. "I'm sure my SUV can navigate the trails."

She might have tried to hide her disappointment, but she was not successful.

"If you will excuse us." Will turned and headed to the office.

"Wow," he said when Nate closed the door behind them, "subtlety is not their strong suit."

Nate chuckled. "Not at all. If you had let Tiffany into your truck, she might have never gotten out until you promised to marry her and live in something other than a tiny tin can."

"Tin can? I'm not going to live in a tin can."

"That's what she called the containers when she was looking through the book with her aunt."

Will shook his head. "Tin cans?"

Nate nodded.

Maybe Tiffany wasn't even the proper realtor to help him sell homes. He didn't doubt her desire to make money. That was obvious from the way she dressed.

"Who wears shoes like that to a construction site?" he grumbled.

"Right?" Nate tipped his head toward the conference room. "Grab your laptop, and let's get busy. We're behind schedule and if we decide to change things up too much, it could be Christmas before we're ready to sell anything."

Which, Will knew, meant that the best time to sell would be over until spring.

CHAPTER 16

"Hey, Barb." Lacey settled into a seat in the Fireside Room at church next to Will's grandmother. She was here, at a lady's small group meeting, at Barb's request. She hoped that the twenty or so ladies who attended this Bible study were as friendly and welcoming as Barb had assured her they were.

"I'm happy you could make it, dear." Barb patted her arm. "Did you have a good day at work?"

"I did, but I think you know that." Barb had been at the library for three of Lacey's eight-hour shift.

Barb darted a look around the room and then, leaning closer to Lacey, whispered, "Did Will show up?"

Lacey nodded. "About half an hour after you left. He had a meeting to get his permit."

"He got it?" Barb's whisper grew a bit louder due to her excitement.

"Shhh," Lacey cautioned. "He did."

"Oh, I am so glad."

That fact was obvious from the way the lady beamed. No one who knew Barb could sanely question her love for her grandkids. It flowed from her in her tone, her words, and even her smile whenever any of them were mentioned.

"Good evening, Barb." A lady in white leggings and a blue and white striped tunic top sat down next to Barb and motioned for an equally stylish younger lady, who was dressed in red denim shorts and a flowy white shirt, to join her. "I don't think you've met my niece, Tiffany."

"No, I haven't. It's a pleasure to meet you, Tiffany. Janice has been looking forward to your arrival, and it seems our prayers have been answered since you are here and all in one piece."

Tiffany laughed. "My aunt is a worrier, isn't she?"

"She is," Barb agreed. "But I think we all are when it comes to people we love." She cast a look at Lacey. "I'd like you to meet a new friend of mine, Janice. This is Lacey Welsh, who is quickly becoming a very dear friend. She may be moving to Hatfield Falls since she just recently landed a job at the library."

"How nice." Janice seemed sincere even if her look was somewhat appraising.

"Will is going to help her find a place if she decides to stay here and not drive back and forth to Marydale," Barb added.

234

"Or I might just stay with my sister for a while," Lacey inserted.

"You have family in Hatfield Falls?" Janice asked.

"Not yet, but I will. Cari moves into her new apartment next week."

"And Cari is your sister?" Tiffany asked.

"Yes."

"Older or younger?"

"Younger."

"Married?"

"No."

"It must be such fun to have a sister." Tiffany's effusion was much too sweet to be genuine in Lacey's opinion. "I don't have any siblings. It's just me."

"But she doesn't lack for friends," Janice inserted, as if being an only child meant one lacked social skills.

"That's good," Lacey said.

"And," Janice continued, "if you need help finding housing, Tiffany is in real estate, and she is exceptional at her job, if I do say so myself."

"I will keep that in mind if I find I need assistance beyond what Will can offer."

"Tiffany is going to be working with Will," Janice said. "We had two very successful meetings with him today." She shared a speaking look with her niece that made Lacey bristle.

"In fact," she continued in a stage whisper, "I think

we made quite a good impression." She winked at Barb. "Maybe one of those grandsons of yours might actually get married."

Barb's eyes grew wide. "You're not trying to pair Will with Tiffany by getting them to work together, are you?"

"All he does is work," Janice protested. "How else am I supposed to do it?"

"Aunt, please." Tiffany's words sounded like they wanted her aunt to stop talking about Will, but her smug expression said the opposite.

"He does not date people he works with," Barb said flatly. "I'm afraid you might have to try another fella for your niece."

"He seemed very welcoming."

"That's called being polite, Janice. He's always very welcoming – especially when it comes to business. He did not get to where he is at such a young age by being rude."

"I suppose you're correct, but Amy thought it might be a good way for Will and Tiffany to meet."

"Amy? My daughter?"

"Yes."

"I still say it won't work."

Lacey turned her phone over and over in her lap as she listened to the two ladies argue over if Will would or would not date Tiffany. With each tick of the school-style clock on the wall at the front of the room, irritation rose an inch higher within Lacey. Will was hers. He was not available for anyone else, and it didn't matter if they worked for him or not. If only he would stop insisting on dating her secretly, then, the annoying discussion taking place beside her would not be happening.

"How did your meeting go?" Mrs. Bennett had finally made her way around the circle of women to where Janice and Tiffany were.

"I thought it went well," Tiffany said. "Will is putting my name on a list of realtors to call for open houses."

"Oh, that's excellent, but did it seem like he might be persuaded to go on a date?" She whispered the last part.

"I would be shocked if he didn't call her," Janice said.

"If you'll excuse me, I'm going to run to the washroom before we start," Lacey said. "Keep my seat for me?" She added to Barb.

"I'll drive them away with my cane," Barb assured her.

"Oh, you can't run away before you give me a hug," Mrs. Bennett said. "Eddie tells me you're settling into your job well."

"I am."

"And do you think he would ask you out?" she added hopefully.

"Even if he did, he wouldn't succeed. Workplace romances are not wise. Things can get awkward at best if they don't work out."

Mrs. Bennett frowned. "I suppose you're right, but who's to say it wouldn't work?"

"Who can guarantee that it would?"

"You have a point, but I do think he's a great guy."

Lacey gave Mrs. Bennett the hug that was required. "I would be shocked if you didn't think so, and you're right. He's a fine gentleman for someone, but not me. Now, if you will excuse me."

She hurried out of the room and down the hall to the ladies' room. Once inside the stall, she took out her phone and tapped on Will's name.

Remember how you told me the other night that you thought it was stupid how the couple in that movie broke up because the heroine overheard something and jumped to conclusions and instead of talking it out, she left in a huff?

She pressed send and then did what she had come to the bathroom to do – other than text Will, that is.

Maaaaybeee? Will replied.

Yes or no, Will. Yes or no.

Yes.

She tucked her phone in her bra and made sure her

clothes were all lying how they should be. Then, she took her phone back out and replied.

This is me not going off in a huff. Tiffany seems to think you're going to ask her out.

You met Tiffany?

And her aunt. Your mother also thinks you might ask Tiffany out.

Where are you?

Ladies meeting at church.

I'm not going to ask anyone out but you. Ever.

Lacey leaned against the stall door. Ever? Was he thinking in forever terms like she was?

You ok? The message popped up on her phone and made her smile.

Yeah. Just a little jealous and annoyed that I have to hide in the bathroom to text you.

Sorry. It's only for a little while.

I know. I still hate it. She bit her lip and paused for three heartbeats before sending the message.

We can go public if you want.

She blew out a breath. There it was again. He would tell everyone he was dating her but only if she asked him to.

I don't want to go public just because I want to go public. I have to go. Someone just came in, and they might need this toilet. TTYL

Ok, but I have no idea what you just said.

She tucked her phone in the pocket of her denim skirt. Why couldn't men understand simple sentences? How could he not get that she wanted *him* to want to be public?

"All set?" Barb asked. Her brow was furrowed with concern.

"Yes," Lacey replied with a smile.

"You look tired."

"I am." Tired of hiding and pretending and telling half-truths.

"You don't have to stay. I know you have a long drive home, and the weather is not great."

Lacey shook her head. "I'm fine. I'm just... tired." She touched her heart and then pretended to rub an itch away.

"Do you want me to talk to you-know-who?"

"No."

"If you ever do..." Barb offered.

"I know. You're very good to me, you know."

Barb smiled. "I do."

Lacey chuckled softly as the meeting got underway.

~*~

Twenty minutes later, as cookies and coffee were being gathered by the ladies, Lacey was even more tired at heart than she had been before the meeting. Mrs. Bennett's teaching tonight had been good. Too good. Because it spoke directly to why her heart was weary. She dug in her bag and pulled out her travel mug.

"Will anyone mind if I fill this and take my coffee to go?" she asked Barb.

"No, not at all, dear. Is something wrong?"

Lacey shook her head. "I just need to ponder what I have heard." And call Will.

Barb grabbed her hand. "I don't like seeing you like this. Are you sure you should leave? We could find a quiet corner in a room somewhere and talk and pray. And maybe the rain will have let up a bit by then."

Lacey blew out a breath. "I need to make a phone call. One that I don't want to make." Tears pricked her eyes. "Will you pray about that for me?"

"Of course, I will. Is this about you and Will?"

Lacey nodded. "We're lying." She shrugged. "You heard the teaching. I can't do that. At least, I can't without hindering my relationship with my heavenly Father."

Barb squeezed her hand. "I knew you were a good one when I met you. Trust God, Lacey. He'll work it out."

Boy, did Lacey hope that was true.

"Are you leaving already?" Janice asked when Lacey was just securing the lid on her travel mug.

"I am. It's not a short drive home." She turned to Mrs. Bennett, who was standing next to Janice.

"Thank you for the meeting. I found it was just what I needed and gave me a lot to consider." She forced a smile. "So, I'll be drinking and thinking while on my way home."

"Drive carefully. That rain is only getting heavier."

"I will." And with those words, she ducked out of the meeting room.

Thanks to the strong wind, the rain was coming down sideways. Her umbrella was going to be of little use. So, Lacey pulled the hood of her jacket tight and ran across the parking lot to her car. Once inside, she gave the vehicle time to defog as she shrugged out of her wet coat and hung it on the back of the seat next to her. She didn't want to wear a wet jacket for forty-five minutes. It could hang there and dry as she drove. If only her skirt could do the same. She pulled a few tissues from the storage compartment on the passenger's side of the car and dried her bare legs, feet, and shoes before buckling up, taking a long sip of coffee, and pressing call on her phone. There was no point in waiting to get this over with.

"Hey, sweetheart," Will answered as she backed out of her parking spot.

"Hi. I'm just heading home from the church." She flipped on the left turn signal and waited for a truck to pass before turning out onto the road.

"Was it a good meeting?" His voice sounded somewhat tense. That was likely due to her final text to him.

"Yeah, it was."

"I'm glad to hear that."

"Your mom is a great teacher." She checked over her shoulder and changed lanes to make her turn onto the country road that would take her to Marydale.

"I have always thought so. Even when I didn't want to hear what she had to teach me."

Was his laugh nervous or was that her projecting her feelings onto everything around her?

"Tonight was one of those lessons."

For a moment, all she heard was the sound of the car's engine, the splash of rain, and the rhythmic slapping back and forth of her windshield wipers.

"How so?" he finally replied.

"It was about integrity and deceit and confidence and insecurity." She blew out a breath. She should have pulled that whole box of tissues out of the compartment and left it on the seat next to her. There was no way she was going to get through what she had to do without a flood of tears that would put the pelting rain to shame.

"I can't do this." She blurted.

"You can't do what?"

"Us. I can't do us. Not as we are doing things."

"You only have to –"

"Let me get this out. Please. It's not easy." Not easy? This was probably the hardest thing she had ever had to do in her life. She sniffled and used the palm of her hand to wipe tears from her cheeks. "I don't want a relationship that is going to require me to compromise my integrity, Will. I want a relationship where my partner trusts me enough to weather the craziness of his family. I want a partner who is secure enough in himself to not need to do everything himself."

"I trust you."

"No, you don't, Will. You trust yourself and what you can control. I get it. I do that, too. I try to control things to keep Cari and myself safe. I did the same with my mom, but as Pastor Anderson has told me, I'm not God. My power to orchestrate life and safety is finite and minuscule." She fumbled to find the tissues she had used to dry her legs without taking her eyes off the road. "I hate that I can't protect her, Will. I hate it. But, I can't not trust God."

"We'll tell everyone we're dating." There was definitely panic in his tone.

"No, we won't. We're not dating." The words tasted bitter in her mouth and made her want to throw up. "Maybe one day we can – one day when you're ready to date someone no matter what your mom does or how suffocating the ladies at church might be. When that day comes, you know where to find me."

"Lacey, wait. I can do that."

"No, you can't. I don't want you to do it just for me, Will. You have to want to do it for yourself because you can't keep your happiness to yourself and need to share it with everyone."

"I can do that." Panic had turned to desperation.

"Goodbye, Will." Wiping her cheeks as quickly as she could with sodden tissues and the palm of her hand could not keep them free of tears. Her heart was shattered and there was no hope of consolation. "I love you," she added before pressing end. It was done.

"Oh, God," she prayed to the emptiness of her car, "let him come back to me. Please, when he's ready, let him come back to me."

CHAPTER 17

Will stared at his phone. She loved him? It didn't feel like it. He tossed his phone on the couch next to him and covered his face with his hands as he slid down so that he could rest his head on the back of that piece of furniture.

How did someone say they loved another person while inflicting pain? He shook his head. None of it made sense. He had told her nearly from the beginning of their relationship that he would tell everyone about them if she wanted him to. Not once had she said she wanted him to end their hiding.

"And somehow, it's my fault?" Anger bubbled up inside him, holding his heart in place instead of letting it crumble as it felt like it was doing.

He uncovered his face. The presentation on the screen of his laptop stared back at him.

"That was a waste of two hours." He hovered his mouse over the x to close the program and considered deleting it, but he couldn't do it. He had put too much work into this slideshow of housing mock-ups and lot allocations, and he still wanted to show it to Lacey. Oh, how he wanted to show it to her and tell her about the new plans that he and Nate had decided on.

His phone chimed, and he snatched it up, hoping that it was Lacey calling him back to say she had made a mistake. But it wasn't Lacey. It was Gran. He tossed it back on the couch. He didn't want to talk to anyone but Lacey.

He let his head flop backward again and he covered his face with his hands once more, pressing against his eyes to keep from crying. It seemed the anger from a moment ago was not strong enough to bury his pain.

"God, why? Why did you let me fail?" he shouted at the ceiling. "What am I supposed to do without her?" he demanded.

The phone next to him chimed again. It was still not Lacey. He tossed it across the room to the basket filled with folded laundry that needed to be put away. He'd let his t-shirts and shorts talk to Gran. He wasn't going to.

The shame of failure washed over him, dripping down his spine, swirling in his gut, squeezing the air from his lungs.

When you're ready to date someone no matter what your mom does...

She didn't understand what his mom would be like. His mom was the sort of mom that made potential girlfriends go running.

It was only one, his conscience prodded.

"Only because I never let her know about any other potential girlfriends," he argued. And it had worked. He had gone out on dates and discovered that he and whomever it was were not right for each other without having the added pressure of his mom's hopes and desires weighing on him. He hated disappointing anyone, but his mom? Well, disappointing her made his heart ache the most. It was a good thing she didn't know about Lacey then, wasn't it?

If she had known, you might not have failed.

"Shut up," he barked at his conscience. "Can't you see I want to feel miserable and justified?"

He was talking to himself. He sighed and attempted to clear his mind of all thoughts. No more thinking for a while. He would sit here and feel all he was feeling and think later when the feelings were done – if they ever were. He began counting because he knew if he didn't use his brain in some way, those unwelcome thoughts would ignore his wishes and poke at him instead of leaving him be.

He had made it all the way to two-hundred thirty-five before the sound of his front door opening stopped his progress.

"He's here, Gran."

"Henry?"

"No, he's not in good shape."

"What are you doing here?" Will demanded.

"Gran was worried about you, and she knew I had a key to your place."

"I'd like that key back," Will grumbled.

"You're not getting it," Henry retorted as he held out his phone to Will. "Gran wants to talk to you."

"I don't want to talk to anyone." Except Lacey.

"Did you hear him?"

Will rolled his eyes.

"Ok." Henry moved the phone from his ear and, after taking a seat in a chair across from the couch, placed the phone on his knee. "You're on speakerphone, Gran."

"No," Will mouthed as he shook his head.

"William Bennett, where is your phone?" Gran demanded.

"In the laundry basket."

"Is it on silent?"

"No."

"Then, why didn't you answer when I called you?"

"I don't want to talk to anyone."

"Well, that's too bad for you," Gran grumbled. "Tell you what. How about if you just listen?"

"Gran!"

"Do not Gran me, William. I am calling because I love you, and I'm one of the only people who know about you and Lacey."

"I watched a movie, Gran. You're not supposed to talk about that."

"Oh, give it a rest, Will. Henry knows. He told me."

Will looked open-mouthed at his brother. Henry didn't tell secrets.

"She was trying to explain why she needed to talk to you immediately, and she was trying her best not to give anything away." He shrugged. "So, I told her I knew, and it doesn't count as giving away a secret if the other person already knows the secret."

"Are you boys quite through being children?" Gran snapped.

"Sorry," Henry said.

Will said nothing.

"William?"

"What?"

"Did she break up with you?"

"Yes."

"Why?" Henry asked.

"Because apparently I don't trust her or anyone except myself and dating me would compromise her integrity." He let his head flop back again.

"She has a point," Henry said.

"Indeed," Gran agreed.

"You can both leave," Will retorted. "I don't need anyone else telling me how horrible I am. I've had quite enough of that." He shook his head. "And do you know what she had the audacity to say before she hung up?"

"No," both Gran and Henry replied.

"That she loves me. *Hi, Will, you're horrible. We can't date, but I love you.*" He knew his voice was dripping with bitterness. Add that to his list of sins.

"She doesn't think you're horrible," Gran said.

"It sure sounded like it."

"And she does love you," Gran added.

Will harumphed in reply. He didn't see how she could.

"If you had cancer, would you want a doctor to pat you on the head, give you a lollipop, and send you on your way as if nothing was wrong, or would you want him to tell you that you had a disease?"

"That's a ridiculous question, Gran." And one he did not want to answer because he knew exactly where this discussion was going.

"No, it's not."

"Just answer the question, Will," Henry said. "It will be less painful."

"Fine," Will said with an exaggerated sigh. "I would want to know I had a disease so that it could be fixed, and you're saying that Lacey told me how horrid I am because I need to be fixed and that proves she loves me. Are we done?"

"Very good." Sarcasm dripped from his grandmother's reply. "Now, what are you going to do to rectify this situation? I can't imagine that you are going to just let the cancer fester until it kills you. And it will. It will kill both you and Lacey."

"Breaking up doesn't kill people, Gran."

"William."

He knew that tone. He had pushed far enough. "Fine. I know what you mean, but that doesn't mean I have to like it."

"No, you don't, but you do have to fix it."

"How? I offered to tell everyone we were dating but that wasn't good enough. She said..." He searched his mind for the correct wording. "She said that she didn't want me to do that for her but for me."

"She's smart," Henry said.

Will rolled his eyes. "So smart that she's given me no way out of this that I can see."

"You'll figure it out," Gran's voice was comforting. "You will figure it out, Will. I have faith in you."

"I'm glad someone does," Will muttered.

"I don't think I'm alone," Gran said. "Now, if you don't mind, I'm going to hang up and call Lacey to check on her. She was in quite the state when she left the church. I can't imagine she got any better on her drive home."

"She was crying," Will admitted.

"She didn't want to make that call, Will. She told me that. She even asked me to pray for her."

Henry tossed Will a box of tissues. "Tears are not confined to the female of the species, Gran."

"Aw, Will, I'm sorry this is so painful."

"Thanks," Will said.

"Henry, give him a hug for me."

"Gran," Henry whined.

"Henry."

Henry sighed. "Stand up, Will."

Will did as Henry said, and Henry gave him a quick squeeze. "I am sorry," he whispered to Will before saying, "Done," to his grandmother.

"Such good boys."

Henry tucked his phone into his pocket.

"What am I going to do?" Will asked him. "I've never failed this bad before."

"You love her, don't you?"

Will nodded. "Yeah, more than I can explain." He shook his head. "You could take my land project and my business and this house and my truck, and all that being gone would not hurt as much."

"Then, start where you should have to begin with." Henry's cheeks puffed out before going flat as he blew out a loud breath. "So this *is* all because of keeping things hidden, right?"

"Yep."

Henry pulled out his phone.

"What are you doing?" Will asked.

Henry only held up a hand to silence him. "Mom? I hurt my ankle falling from a ladder after sneaking into Blake and Tyler's place to play a prank on Tyler." Henry covered the speaker on his phone. "Hey, I'm a quick study. I'm not going to let my integrity get questioned by Lacey."

"No, Mom. I did not say I wanted to date Lacey. ... Yes, Mom, I know that sneaking into houses is not right. You do know I am an adult, right? ... Right. Adults do not play childish pranks. Got it. I love you and will not sneak into Tyler's house again. ...Who else's house do you think I would sneak into? ... No, I'm not going to sneak into any houses, Mom. I'm at Will's. ... Yep, we'll see you on Sunday." He gave Will a questioning look to which Will nodded in answer. "Mm-hmm. Yep. I'll tell him."

"Tell me what?" Will asked when Henry had hung up.

"She loves you, and she'd like to know how your meeting with Tiffany went."

Will groaned.

"Who's Tiffany?"

"Mrs. Martin's high-maintenance and annoying niece, who happens to be a realtor and who Mom thought I could help get established in real estate here in Hatfield Falls."

"High-maintenance you say?"

Will nodded. "Just ask Nate about the ridiculous shoes she wore to our construction office."

Henry laughed. "Is she pretty?"

Will shrugged. "I guess."

"Not as pretty as Lacey, eh?"

"Something like that." Will smiled sadly.

"Are you going to be ok?"

"Yeah, I'll survive. Thanks for bringing Gran over." He moved toward the door, and Henry followed.

"Are you sure you're actually glad about that? You didn't seem too happy when I got here."

"I'm glad. I wasn't happy. I'm still not, but I needed it." He shook his head. "Do I really only trust myself?"

His brother grimaced, and Will knew the answer before Henry gave it. "You kinda do, bro."

"Nate said something like that, too, earlier."

"Hey, it's easy to do, especially when you're as smart and ambitious as you are."

Will shook his head. "Doesn't make it right."

"No, it doesn't, but it does make it understandable. You know what Dad says. We all have our own designer-made weaknesses." Henry paused at the door. "You know my number if you need anything. Anything. I promise not to breathe a word of this to anyone – except Gran because she's Gran."

"Thanks." Will made sure the door was locked and Henry had gotten to his car before he turned off the entryway light and went back to the living room.

What was he going to do to win Lacey back? He rubbed the back of his neck. He had no clue. Not one single idea. However, he did know who might be able to help him.

After retrieving his phone from the laundry basket, he settled onto the couch and propped his feet on the coffee table next to his laptop, which had gone to sleep.

"Hi, Dad," Will said when his dad answered the phone. "Is Mom home?"

"She's here. What's up?"

"I messed up, Dad." Wow, that wasn't quite as painful to say as he had thought it might be. Still, it didn't feel good. "Bad. Like I've never messed up before."

"Oh, well, do you want to talk to me about it or does this need your mom?"

"You guys alone?"

"Yeah, Emma just went home."

"Then, can you put me on speakerphone so I can talk to both of you?"

"Sounds serious."

"It is."

"Amy, Will needs to speak to us. Do you have a few minutes?"

Will listened to the shuffling sounds of people moving as he waited.

"Ok, she's here in the living room with me on the couch. Now, what's all this about?" His dad asked. "He says he's messed up on something," his dad added as an explanation to his mom.

"Lacey and I have been dating. Secretly. Until tonight when she told me that doing so was compromising her integrity and broke up with me. Mom, I don't know how to fix it, but I need to because I love her."

CHAPTER 18

The rain had stopped.

That was the first thought that entered Lacey's mind as she slowly began to grasp her surroundings. The windshield wipers squeaked as they dragged themselves across the no-longer-rain-covered glass.

It was dark. Not just dusky, but dark.

That was Lacey's second thought that was quickly followed by a third.

Everything hurt. Some parts of her hurt more than other parts, but everything hurt to some degree.

She reached around the airbag and turned off the wailing wipers.

"Ow!"

Turning off those wipers did not take much effort, but it was enough to send searing pain up her arm. She breathed deliberately through her teeth as she moved her arm to find her phone.

"Oooooh." She moaned as she pulled the phone

from its holder and brought it to where she could see it, propping it on the deflated bag in front of her.

She leaned back and breathed deeply as the pain subsided a bit when her arm was still. She allowed her right arm to rest on her leg and used her left hand to open her contacts list. The words swam in front of her eyes. She squeezed her eyes shut and blinked when she opened them, but the blurriness did not go away.

That was alright. She could do this without being able to read the words clearly. Two down was Cari. She pressed the call contact button, followed by the speaker icon, and waited.

"Lacey?"

"Will?" She squinted at the phone screen. Two down was Cari. Three down was Will. "I'm sorry. I was trying to call Cari, but I'm having trouble seeing my phone."

"Where's Cari? Isn't she home with you? And why are you having trouble seeing your phone?"

Lacey moaned. "I'm not home."

"What's wrong?"

She could hear a hint of panic in his voice, but he seemed to be rather calm.

"Something ran out in front of my car." Oh, her head was throbbing, and her neck was aching. She blew out a breath. "The good news is, I missed it. The bad news is, I went off the road. Oh," she moaned, "airbags hurt."

"Where are you?"

Cool calmness, like when the doctor needed you to remain calm and modulated his voice to project what he wanted to create in your mind, coloured Will's tone. Lacey was grateful for it. She was struggling as it was to not listen to her anxiety.

"I'm not exactly sure. I sort of remember seeing that place where Emma and Cari bought the bus."

"She's gone off the road. Call emergency." She heard Will say to someone in the room with him. There were several voices that answered him.

"Where are you?" she asked.

"I'm at Mom and Dad's."

"Oh, ok."

"Mom is calling for help."

"Thank you."

"And Dad is calling Cari and then Gran."

"Why Barb?" Cari, she understood, but why would Pastor Bennett think Barb needed to know about her accident?

"She's been trying to call you and not getting an answer. She was going to call Cari if she didn't get you to answer soon."

"Oh, ok." She sighed. "I hurt, Will. All over."

"I'm sorry, sweetheart. Help is coming."

"Take care of Cari."

"We will make sure your sister is safe. Keep talking to me."

"About what? Thinking kind of hurts." Sleep sounded good. Maybe if she could just go to sleep this pain would stop.

"How long ago did your accident happen?"

"I don't know. It was raining, and now, it's not."

"At least twenty minutes ago," Will said to someone. "Mom needed to know for the emergency services," he explained to her.

"Ok."

"Do you know anything else about where you are?"

"Let me look." Lacey turned her head and cried out.

"Don't move." Will's voice was firm and almost harsh. "They'll find you. Do you have your lights on?"

"Yes."

"Any chance you can turn on your four-way flashers?"

"No. I don't want to move that arm. It hurts too much."

"Injured right arm," Will said to his mom. "Is it broken?" he asked Lacey.

"I think so. Will, tell them to hurry." She wasn't sure how much longer she could keep her emotions intact and not listen to her fear, which was trying its best to make her consider all the catastrophic things that could happen.

"They'll be there as fast as they can be."

"I'm tired, and I hurt. And..." she paused. "I'm scared," she whispered.

"I'm sorry, sweetheart."

She tried to wrap the comfort in his words around her heart. It was as if she hadn't been cruel to him however long ago it was now. It hadn't been that long ago.

"Hang on, sweetheart. You're going to be ok."

A new worry crept into her mind at his words.

"Why are you calling me that?" Calling her sweetheart was not going to keep his parents in the dark about their former relationship, and he was at their house.

"Because I love you."

That was going to do even less to conceal things. "But your parents..."

"They know everything. That's why I'm here. I called them, but then, Mom said it would be better if I just came over to discuss what I can do to fix me – to fix us?"

"Wait. Did you say you love me?"

"Yes, and I don't want a life without you, Lacey, and I don't care who knows that."

"Oh, Will." She wanted to just run to him with

open arms, but she also needed to know that he wasn't just doing this because he thought she wanted him to do it.

"Hey, I know it's too soon for you to trust me on that. I know I need to earn it, and I will."

"Forgiveness or grace or whatever the right thing is that you think you need to earn can't be earned, Will."

He chuckled. She loved that sound and the man who made it. "Mom will be pleased to know that even when in pain you can still scold me."

She tried to laugh. "Ribs are too sore to laugh."

He passed that information on to his mom and then returned to her. "Forgiveness and grace cannot be earned, but trust can be. I intend to prove to you that I trust you and others and not just myself."

"And God? Do you trust Him?" That was the most important.

"Yeah, yeah, I do. Dad and I were just talking about that when Gran called. Oh, Emma's here. She has Cari on her phone. Hold on while I have Emma hang up and then add Cari to this call."

Lacey's phone went silent for a minute while Will added Cari to his call.

"Lacey?"

She breathed a sigh of relief at hearing her sister's voice. "Hi, Cari. We're going to need to go car shopping soon."

"Are you hurt?"

"I am."

"Bad?"

"I don't know, but I'm going to say medium."

"Medium?"

"Yep, not small and not deadly – somewhere in the middle. I love you."

"I love you, too."

"I love you, too, Lacey," Will inserted.

"Are you eavesdropping, Will?"

"Yep. Absolutely."

"Hang on, you love my sister?" Cari asked.

"I sure do, and I hope to date her properly at some point."

"What do you mean date her properly?"

There was a bite to Cari's tone. As much as Lacey looked out for Cari, Cari returned the favour in her own way.

"Until tonight, we'd been dating secretly. It was totally my idea, and I talked her into it. So don't be mad at her."

"It didn't take much talking. The kissing helped," Lacey said.

"You kissed my sister?"

"Several times."

"Where's Emma?" Cari asked.

"Behind me," Will answered. "Do you want to talk to her instead of Lacey?"

"No. But you can tell her the cinnamon buns worked."

"Cinnamon buns?" both Will and Lacey said together.

"Why do you think we kept sending you to drop off cinnamon buns to Will and Nate?" Cari asked.

"Emma, Cari says to tell you the cinnamon buns worked," Will said.

"I see flashing lights," Lacey said over the top of whatever Emma had said in reply. "What did she say?"

"She said 'I guess Cari was right that you'd make a good couple.'"

"We broke up. We're not a couple," Lacey retorted.

"But you will be," Cari assured her.

"They're here," Lacey said as a fire truck pulled up alongside her. It wasn't the really long one with the ladders and hoses but one of the shorter ones.

"We'll let you go then, and we'll see you at the hospital," Will said. "Have them tell us if you go to somewhere other than the medical center here in Hatfield Falls."

"I will."

"I love you, Lacey," Will said.

"Love you, too," she replied.

266

"See, you can't say that and not be a couple," Cari inserted before adding her own I love you for her sister and a promise to bring clothes to the hospital.

Lacey pushed the button to lower the window and was grateful both for the fact that the car was still on so it would lower and that the button was accessible to her left hand.

"Hi, there, Miss Welsh?" A first responder stood at her door. "We're going to get you out of there, I heard it mentioned that your neck hurts?"

"Only when I turn it or try to move. I don't think it is broken." She really hoped it wasn't. "I can wiggle my toes and I can feel my arms"

He smiled at her and the skin around his eyes crinkled into several lines that made him appear exceptionally friendly. "I'm happy to hear that, but, just in case, I'm still going to ask you to stay very still until we have this somewhat unpleasant collar on you. I promise you that it will make moving you a little less painful."

"Thank you."

He picked her phone up off the airbag and handed it to a guy behind him. "Make sure that gets to the ambulance along with any other personal effects."

"Are you ready?" he asked Lacey.

She closed her eyes, drew a breath while saying a

quick prayer for strength and protection, and then said, "Yes. Please, get me out of here."

~*~

"You have visitors," a sweet older nurse named Denise stuck her head into Lacey's room the next morning. "I told them that they have to wait until I have checked all I need to check and make sure you're decent." She winked. "That Will is pretty handsome. I've known him since he was a baby in the nursery at church."

"Do you go to church with the Bennetts?"

"I do, but my schedule here keeps me away for a minimum of two Sundays per month." She pushed the button on the blood pressure machine and flipped up the blanket to check the catheter bag. Then, she took out her pen and jotted things down on Lacey's chart.

"You're doing well. Dr. Ling will be in to see you later and give you a little brain test and all that." She bustled around getting what she needed to do done.

"If Dr. Ling says it's ok, we'll see if we can't get rid of some of these attachments later," Denise said as she checked the IV bag. "Will seems sweet on you."

Lacey felt her cheeks flush. "He is." She remembered his intense look when he had told her last night that he'd prove to her that he wanted her in his life.

"And is it mutual? I kind of hope it is since he's telling everyone out there that you're his girlfriend."

"It is, but we've hit a little bit of a snag that we need to work through."

Denise patted her thigh. "What couple doesn't hit those now and then?"

Lacey knew it was true, but the thought did nothing to calm her. There was still a serious discussion that she and Will needed to have before she would feel completely at peace about him claiming her as his girlfriend. She needed to hear his heart, to know that he wasn't just attempting to please her.

"Oh, now, look what I did. You're nervous."

It was hard to hide that fact when the machine next to you was beeping out your heartbeats.

She took Lacey's hand. "I don't do this with everyone, and I'd likely get in trouble if my supervisor knew I had done it, but..." She closed her eyes. "Father, I'm lifting Lacey up to you. She needs your peace and healing. Wrap her in your love."

Her eyes opened again. "I do that a lot actually. It's just that I usually do it silently while pretending to take a pulse or something. But I thought you needed to hear the words."

Lacey's heart rhythm fell back into a steady close-to-regular pace, and Denise flipped a switch.

"We do not need this contraption alerting Mrs.

Bennett to how much you like her son." She winked. "Besides, you don't need it on constantly now anyway. We'll check periodically. Shall I send them in?"

"Please."

"Hope you like flowers," she said as she ducked out of the room.

"I see you have Denise taking care of you," Mrs. Bennett said as she entered the room ahead of Will, Cari, and Emma. Each of them was carrying a vase of flowers. "She's fantastic."

She came to the side of the bed and looked down at Lacey. "Oh, my, you do look like you've gone a couple of rounds with a prizefighter." Then, she bent and kissed her forehead just like Lacey's mom used to do when Lacey was ill. "We need to talk, but I'll let your sister and Will have their time first. Oh, it's nothing horrible. I promise," she added when Lacey's eyes went wide.

"Did you sleep well?" Cari asked.

She, Emma, and Will had stayed at the hospital as late as they possibly could last night. In fact, they had been discussing taking turns sitting vigil with her until Lacey had begged them to just go home and sleep. Who wanted to have someone staring at them while they were sleeping? Not her. That was just creepy.

"I did. Those pain meds they gave me were knock-outs. Literally."

"Good. Any news on when you get to break free from here?"

"I won't know until the doctor visits this afternoon, but I think I might be here one more night."

"Has your vision cleared?"

"Yeah, it has."

"Barb said she'd be by later if you were still here."

"I think she's planning to sneak in some cookies for you," Emma inserted. "She claims no one can heal properly without some treats."

"She is a dear." Lacey blinked at the tears that gathered.

"What's wrong?" Cari asked.

"Nothing. I just feel loved and am on pain meds."

"You are loved," Will inserted.

"Will won't let us forget that," Emma whispered. "He keeps repeating it."

"Hey, it's true," Will said.

"But we know it already. You don't have to keep telling us."

"I want to," he said while holding Lacey's gaze. "I can't stay right now, but tonight, if you're still here, I'll be back so we can talk if you're up for it."

"I'd like that."

He playfully pushed his sister and hers out of the

way so that he could get close enough to kiss her fore-head. "I truly do love you." He gave her a small smile. "If you're not here tonight, I'll come visit you wher-ever you are, or we can talk on the phone, ok?"

Though his actions seemed to be those of a man who was sure of his standing with her, his look and tone said otherwise, and that touched her heart more deeply than any declaration of love could. One could say words and make them sound good. Her father had been good at that. It was much harder to let those words show in an anxious look and cautious tone. He loved her and not just because she wanted him to. She knew it, and it filled her heart with the peace she had been longing for.

"She'll be at my place," Cari said.

"Oh, that's right! The apartment is ready."

"Completely ready?" Lacey asked in surprise. It wasn't supposed to be ready yet.

"No," Will answered, "but ready enough for you to stay there."

"If we can get you up the stairs," Cari added.

"Henry offered to rig up a pulley on the deck to hoist you up," Emma said with a laugh.

"I hope you told him no!"

"Of course, we did. It was just Henry being Henry," Emma assured her. "We're going over there now to make sure that everything you need is in place for whenever you are released."

"Tonight?" Will asked.

Lacey smiled. "Tonight."

Mrs. Bennett escorted her children and Cari from the room and then returned to Lacey's bedside. She pulled a chair close and took a seat. Then, she blew out a breath and said, "I'm sorry."

Lacey blinked. "For what?"

"For being overly exuberant about my son finding a wife." She grimaced. "I haven't gone completely nuts since that first time Will brought a girl to a church activity, but that incident stuck. And my constant inquiries about who he was dating or my suggestions about who to consider did nothing to help rid him of that fear of failing in a relationship. I am why he did what he did." She sighed deeply. "I'd like to tell you that I will never be overbearing again, but I can't. I will try, and I would ask you to tell me if I am being over the top. Would you be my accountability sister in that?"

"Me?"

"Yes. You know best the harm that I can do." She took a tissue from the little box on the bedside table and dabbed at her eyes. "Will you help me with this?"

"Of course, but you're a pastor's wife." Did pastor's wives really need accountability partners other than

273

their husbands? She had never really thought about it before, but she supposed they did. But shouldn't that partner be someone older and wiser than Lacey was?

"Pastor's wives are just regular women married to men who have been called by God to lead a flock of believers. We do not automatically become perfect. I wish we did." She shook her head. "I'm so sorry. Will loves you. So much. I saw it in his broken-hearted plea for help last night. He hasn't laid his heart open like that for me since he was in grade school."

She dabbed at her eyes again. "He would not thank me for saying this I am sure since he feels that he must prove himself and he's always been rather independent, but he's not shouting his love for you from the rooftops because he's trying to please you." She shook her head again to emphasize her words. "He's truly repentant. I've known him long enough to know what that looks like, and believe me, the Will you saw last night and today is a truly repentant and humbled man."

"Can I have one of those tissues?" Lacey asked.

"Aw, sweetie, I didn't mean to make you cry." Mrs. Bennett propped the tissue box on Lacey's abdomen.

"Calling him last night was the hardest thing I have ever done, but after your lesson, I knew we weren't pleasing God. I'm sorry I let him talk me into hiding our relationship. He's not solely at fault. I know that."

"I'm glad you called him. I know that it broke your heart and his, but it was necessary. There is nothing left to forgive. Is there?"

Lacey saw the same anxious expression Will had worn earlier in his mother's eyes and again felt the love that it imparted. "No, there's nothing left to forgive for you or Will."

Mrs. Bennett's smile was bright, though her lips did tremble some as she dried her eyes again. "Since we have that out of the way. I knew that this room had a DVD player – because I asked – and I brought my collection of Austen adaptations. I thought we could watch an episode together until you got sleepy." She pulled three boxes out of her bag. "Which will it be?"

Lacey gasped. "You have the *Emma* one with Johnny Lee Miller?"

Mrs. Bennett beamed. "I most certainly do. Would you like to watch it?"

"Oh, yes, please."

Mrs. Bennett put the rest of her collection back in the bag and then went to try to figure out how to run the DVD player while Lacey settled back on her pillows and thanked God for bringing Will back to her before he was really even gone.

CHAPTER 19

"I'm going to mess up," Will said as he pulled into traffic just as the sun was beginning to slip below the horizon.

Dr. Ling had decided to release Lacey instead of making her stay another night, but he hadn't done so until well after supper. That meant that Will and Lacey had not yet had a chance to talk, and it was not that far from the hospital to Cari's place. Therefore, Will plunged in at the crux of the issue – his failure.

"I really hate that fact," he continued. "Like, more than you can imagine, but it's true. I promise to do my best, but I am going to make mistakes, Lacey."

He glanced at her to see how she was responding to his admission. She had turned her body to look at him rather than just her head, and her expression registered her surprise in lifted eyebrows and wide eyes. He put a hand on hers.

"Both hands on the wheel if you don't mind," she said with a small smile.

He gave her hand a squeeze and returned his hand to the steering wheel as she had requested. He was certain she would be a little skittish about driving or riding in vehicles for a while after what she had been through.

"You kind of just jumped right in there," she said. "Headfirst."

"I've been thinking of little else since you called me last night."

"I'm sorry I didn't let you talk then." She blew out a breath. "I don't do well with arguments."

"I know they make you nervous. Remember, I saw it at the library that day?" How long ago that day seemed now even though it had only been about a month ago. However, yesterday seemed to be a month long all by itself.

"I remember."

"I wish you had let me talk." Although it may not have done him as much good as being forced to face his shortcomings with the help of others had.

"I'm sorry. I'll work on that."

That was a hopeful thing. If she was going to work on something it meant she was truly going to keep him around, didn't it?

"And I'll work on my control issues. You aren't the

first person to mention them to me." He fell silent as they pulled up to a red light. "Nate is my business partner, and I tend to second guess or double-check everything he does. Not very trusting, huh?" He glanced at her. "And Nate and I've been friends since I was eight."

She was still looking at him with that small smile that he found both comforting and encouraging.

"Your mom said you have always had an independent spirit that likes to make sure things are done right."

"She did? When was that?"

"When we were watching *Emma* yesterday. By the way, she owns my favourite one."

"Is that what she had in her bag yesterday?"

"Yep, along with some movie snacks."

He chuckled. That sounded like his mom. She was good at hosting events – big or small.

"I really like her, Will."

He shot Lacey a smile. "I do, too, even if it hasn't seemed like I do. But back to what I was saying." He glanced at her again to see if she was ok with returning to the topic of discussion that needed to happen. She did not look away or even move to say something.

"I will mess up, but I need you to not walk away when I do." He knew that was asking a lot of her with her history with her father causing her to be nervous about disagreements and such. "Of course, I want you to tell me when I'm being stupid, but I don't want a future without you."

He pulled his truck to the side of the street. They were only a few blocks away from the apartment now.

"*I, me,*" he pointed at himself as he turned toward her. "I don't want a future without you. I am changing my ways not just for you, but also for me. There is no way for me to take you out of my motivation because you are my motivation. I need you."

How else did he describe what he felt for her? He was not even sure he could explain it to himself. There was just this void that she filled and that he hadn't known he had until she came into his life, and he never again wanted to feel as empty as he had when she had said goodbye to him yesterday.

"I can't explain it any better than that, Lacey. Will you give me a chance to prove to you that I am not just words? Please. I'm so sorry I ever asked you to hide our relationship."

She held her left hand out to him, and he took it. "I'm sorry I let you talk me into it."

He kissed her hand. "You followed my lead. I led you wrong. I am more at fault."

"I'm not going to argue about who is more at fault, Will." Her gaze was piercingly serious. "What I'm going to do is tell you what I told your mom when she apologized to me."

Will blinked. "Mom apologized to you?"

Lacey gave a very small nod of her head, one that would not cause her neck to hurt. Small movements, she had said, were ok. Larger movements were the ones that caused her pain.

"She did, and when we were done talking about it, I told her that there was nothing left for me to forgive for her or you."

His eyebrows drew together. "You forgave me based on her apology?"

"Yeah."

He leaned back and stared out the windshield while still holding Lacey's hand. "Wow. Dad would like that for a sermon illustration," he said with a small chuckle.

"What do you mean?"

"I was granted forgiveness based on what someone else did. That sounds a lot like what happens with salvation." A lot like it. He blew out a breath. "Wow," he said again. "That makes grace pretty real." He looked at her as feelings he had never experienced before like he was right now – peace, gratefulness, and joy – washed over him.

"I guess you're right," she agreed.

"It's like you said on the phone after your accident.

I don't have to earn it." Of course, he had still felt like he had to, but now? Now he didn't, and that part of his father's sermon repertoire about the Christian life being lived as an act of gratitude for the grace and forgiveness that had been freely given seemed so much more real than it ever had before.

He kissed the back of her hand again. "Thank you."

Her brow furrowed. "For what?"

"For helping me understand who God is better than I did before."

Her brow remained furrowed. "You're welcome?"

He laughed. "I assure you that it's a good thing and that I have not lost my mind." He held her gaze. "Are we ok?"

That removed her look of confusion and replaced it with a smile. "Yeah, we're ok."

"So, I haven't been lying to everyone when I've been telling them you are my girlfriend?"

She laughed as he put his truck into gear and signalled to pull away from the curb.

"About that. It seems rather presumptuous of you to do."

Oh, he agreed, and his heart had quivered each time he had said it because he knew full-well that he might be setting himself up for a humiliating failure if she turned him away. Be that as it may, it had to be done.

"I wanted to show you that I was willing to claim you as mine when there was a lot for me to lose," he explained, "and it was the only thing I could think of to show you that I was serious about wanting us."

"I'd shake my head at you if it wouldn't hurt so much," she said.

"I was desperate. I could have lost you twice yesterday. First, when you broke up with me, and then, when your car crashed – it could have been so much worse than it was." He had seen the crumpled car this morning, and even though Lacey had cuts, bruises, and a broken arm, he knew that God had protected her from greater or even fatal injuries.

"I'm so glad I didn't," he admitted aloud.

"So am I," she replied, allowing him to remove his hand from the steering wheel to give hers a squeeze without saying a word about it but rather squeezing his fingers in return.

It was a little action, but it let him know that they were fine and likely better than they had been before the accident. He said a quiet word of thanks to God for the gift of the woman next to him, and then, as he turned into the parking lot at the Evans Street apartment building, he said, "Now, for what I've been working on all day today with Cari and Emma. Your room is all ready for you. The bed is made, clothes are in the closet and dresser, towels in the bathroom, everything is done."

"It's all done?"

"Every bit." It had been a busy day, but he was used to pushing to get a house ready for an open house, so it wasn't like he had never staged a room in record time before.

He pulled into the parking spot labelled for visitors.

"Don't even try to get out by yourself," he said as he turned off the truck. "I'm carrying you."

"I can walk."

"Not tonight, sweetheart. The doctor was pretty clear that you're to take it easy for a few days before trying too much." And it would be at least a week before she would be cleared to return to work part-time.

"Walking is not too much," she called after him as he got out.

"I could let you walk across the parking lot, but it will be easier for me to lift you from the truck than it will be from the ground. Those steps are going to be a challenge on your own. Do you think you can slide across to my side of the truck? I need your left arm to go around my neck."

"You expect me to climb over this?" She pointed to the center console. "I think walking would be easier."

He frowned, but she had a point. "I don't like it."

"Will, please. I know you want to make sure I'm well, but I can walk. I walked out of the hospital."

He sighed. "Fine. But wait for me to help you from the truck."

"That, I can do."

~*~

Will was standing with his father in the church foyer when Lacey walked into church three weeks later. They had been hanging out at Cari's or Emma's or even his parent's house nearly every day since her accident. She had returned to work two weeks ago, and next week, she was going to try three half-days and two full-days instead of doing five half-days. Her arm was still in a cast and sling, but her bruises had faded, and she moved less stiffly than she had that night he had taken her home to her sister's place from the hospital. However, her sunglasses were still never too far from her so she could dim the lights for her head's sake when needed.

Today, they would hang out at the church picnic, which was set to take place out on the lawn in about an hour. A group of ladies were in the kitchen now getting things ready, and a few men were outside firing up the barbeques that had been brought to the parking lot for today. The Bennett clan, along with a few others like Nate and his mom, were in the church foyer talking as they waited to be summoned to the lawn.

Lacey saw him and smiled before heading towards his mother and Gran. He wasn't sure why he had ever thought that Lacey wouldn't be able to handle his mother when she and Gran had become friends so quickly. It was as if God had dropped the perfect woman into his life.

No, it wasn't *as if*. God *had* dropped the perfect woman into his life, and while she had only been in his life for a couple of months now, today, he was hopefully going to make certain she was always in his life.

"And now, we are going to lose Will's attention," Henry quipped.

"The work will get done," Will said, returning his attention to the group of men he was standing with. "All Nate and I need is your list of needs, right?"

"That's it," Nate agreed.

The church had recently voted to refresh the youth wing. He and Nate were donating their time to oversee the project.

"See. I told you." Henry teased as Will headed toward Lacey.

"Leave him be," he heard his dad say. "He's got important things to do."

His dad was one of two people who knew about

what Will had planned, and that was only because Will had stopped in at his dad's office to let him in on it.

"Like what?" Henry asked.

That was his middle brother – curiosity personified.

"Why don't you come find out," Will called to him. "I promise it will be good."

Or at least he hoped it would be. This putting himself into places where failure taunted him from the sidelines was not yet getting any easier than it had been three weeks ago when he had begun to challenge himself about it by calling Lacey his girlfriend when she had not yet given him a second chance. Hopefully, if this went well, he'd be able to call her something better than girlfriend.

"Good morning," he whispered as he slipped between her and his mom.

"Morning," she whispered back. "Do you have the presentation done?"

She knew that he had decided to finish the presentation about the new development plans and show it to his mom when it was done. The last time she had seen it, it had been almost complete. There had only been a few secret changes to make to it before presenting it. He was pretty sure she would not mind him being secretive about those changes, such as a

287

larger owner's house attached to the office, one that was large enough for a family.

"Good morning," Mrs. Clark said to him when the conversation the ladies were having about Emma's and Cari's first Saturday at the farmer's market with their food truck lapsed for a moment shortly after he arrived. "Nate said there is a hard and firm date for the open house."

"Indeed, there is. The foundation is in place and tomorrow, the containers for the office and house structure arrive. Then, Nate assures me that it will only be a few weeks until it is ready to welcome you and others."

"I'll be looking for my invitation."

"It will be among the first we send out," he assured her.

"Along with mine," Gran inserted.

"That goes without saying," Will said.

"No, it doesn't. I need to hear these things." His grandmother winked at him.

Will shook his head. She did like to be demanding even when it was not needed.

"Speaking of the open house and the development. I got new brochures." He pulled one out of his back pocket. "Do you want to see it?"

"Oh, you know I do," Gran said.

"I do, too," his mother agreed.

"Pass it around," Mrs. Clark said.

He handed the brochure to his mom.

She gasped. "You named it!"

"I was getting tired of referring to it as 'the development.'"

"What's the name?" Emma asked. She gave Will a look that said she was not happy that he had been holding back this information.

"Yes, what is it?" Lacey asked. That seemed to make Emma feel better that she did not know about the name. No one but Nate new about that name.

"Jayni Landing."

"Jayni?" Emma's eyebrows shot up in surprise. "That seems like a random name."

Will shook his head. "It's not. I had to research to find it. It means *Jehovah has shown favour*, and while it's not *Pemberley Shores*, it does nod to the creator of Pemberley."

"Jane Austen?" Edmund asked. Apparently, the whole group of men had followed Will over to join the ladies.

"Yep. For Mom."

His mom's hand flew to her heart, and tears sprang to her eyes. "That's lovely. All of it. These models look fabulous."

"Those are Nate's work." That was also part of Will's plan to learn to trust someone other than himself, and while he might sound nonchalant about it at present, it had not been, and still wasn't, easy. But it was worth it.

"Oh, look at the names of the places," Mrs. Clark said with a smile for Will. "The Maggie, Katie Place, Abbey Court," she read three of the names. "Do I correctly suspect some more Austen influence?"

"That was also Nate's idea." Nate had thought playing on names found in Jane Austen's novels would be a fun way to extend the theme of the community's name.

"This is a long way from not wanting to have anything to do with Austen," Henry said from where he stood looking at the brochure over Mrs. Clark's shoulder.

"Love makes men do things they might not otherwise do," his dad replied. "At least, that's my guess."

Will swallowed and nodded. "It does."

"Well, I think it's wonderful." His mom could not look prouder, he was sure of it, but he was not done delighting her. At least, he hoped he wasn't done.

"Say, Lacey," he began, "I know we've been dating for a while, but we haven't been able to go out for a real dinner yet. I was wondering if you'd like to do that?" His heart picked up its pace, and he tried to surreptitiously dry the palms of his hands on his jeans.

"Go out for dinner?" Her cheeks were a lovely

shade of light pink. Her eyes darted around the group of people before returning to him. She probably thought it was odd that he would ask her to dinner in such a large group. Honestly, it felt weird.

"Yeah, will you have dinner with me?"

She blinked and gave a half shrug. "Sure, I'd like to have dinner with you. When?"

He slipped his hand into his pocket and hooked the item he had hidden in there with his finger. "Forever." He pulled his hand out of his pocket and held a sparkly diamond ring out to her.

There was a collective gasp around him, but he only had eyes for the woman in front of him who held his happiness in her control. She looked at the ring and then, at him.

"Are you -?" Her question fell away without being completed as if the words were too much for her brain to process as she looked back at the ring.

"Will you marry me, Lacey?"

Her eyes returned to him.

"Maybe in December? I hear December weddings are beautiful."

"Four months from now?"

He hadn't thought her eyes could get wider.

"Or in the spring," he said. "Or the summer. Or next autumn. I really don't care when our wedding is.

I only care that you are by my side for life. What do you say?"

Slowly her startled expression slid into one of happiness. "Can we have a tower of cinnamon buns instead of a cake?"

"As long as they don't have raisins in them. Is that a *yes*?"

Her head bobbed up and down. "Yes! It is most definitely a *yes*." She held her left hand out for him to put the ring on her finger.

"It fits perfectly, and it's just what I would have chosen," she said as she admired it.

"Cari helped me get it right."

"You knew about this?" Lacey asked her sister.

"Yeah, I knew."

"Thank you." She gave Cari a half-hug since her right arm was still not useable.

"I can't believe this," Lacey said, admiring her ring again.

"Oh, for heaven's sake," Gran said. "Kiss the girl already."

The rest of the group laughed, and Will pulled Lacey to him.

"You don't like the public proposals in the movies we have watched," she whispered.

"Love makes a man do things he wouldn't normally

do," he answered. "And I do love you, Lacey. Forever and always. And I don't care who knows."

He lowered his lips to hers, planning to give her just a sweet and chaste kiss, but success was not to be his.

However, as his arms wrapped around her and held her close and his kiss moved quickly and naturally from sweet to something stronger, he decided that this was one failure that he could more than live with. He could relish it, revel in it, and hope to have it happen again and again. But then, as he had been learning, failure did not always mean the end of something. Sometimes, it meant the beginning of something so much better than he could have ever imagined.

CHAPTER 20: A STEP TOWARDS NEW BEGINNINGS

The heroine of Hatfield Falls (Don't Tell) book 2 is Lacey's and Edmund's co-worker, Trish Thomspon. Here's a little scene set at an apple orchard on Canadian Thanksgiving (which is in early October) to help us get to know her better.

Trish pulled her jacket down so that it would lay as it was supposed to do – with the hem at the top of her thighs – instead of bunching at her waist like it always did when she was driving. She stashed her purse in the trunk of her vehicle after making sure that she had all the important things, such as lip balm, tissues, and money, stuffed in her pockets.

"Hey, do I know you?"

"Ow!" Trish rubbed the spot on the back of her head that had crashed into the still open hatchback when she jumped.

"Sorry. I didn't mean to surprise you. I thought you would have heard me." A sheepish grin graced a face that did look familiar in a rugged, unshaven sort of way.

She slammed the hatchback closed because if you didn't give it a good slam, it often did not catch and would not lock. "Are you a Bennett?" she asked the source of the slight throbbing in her head.

"I am. Brandon, son number two of five."

She stuck out her hand. "Trish Thompson. I work with Eddie."

"Ah, so that's probably where I've seen you."

She didn't know when because she would have remembered if she had seen him. He had a disarming smile. What was it about those Bennett boys that made them so irresistible? His grip as he shook her hand was firm. Those were not the hands of a pencil pusher.

"So, a book nerd, eh?"

"Guilty as charged," she answered with a laugh. "And what do you do?"

He patted the bag at his side. "Camera geek."

"Yeah? That's cool. What kind of photography do you do?"

"Nature stuff mainly, but I can do portraits and business pictures as well. I just would rather work with animals than humans."

"Not the social sort?"

He shrugged. "When I need to be, but no, not really."

He was honest. She had to give him that.

"Are you here for this activity?" she asked as they both began walking toward the entrance to the apple orchard.

"Only because my mother insisted that she needed pictures of Will and Lacey. Otherwise, I'd be on a hike somewhere."

"You really are into nature, aren't you?"

"Oh, yeah. I love it."

"Then, I suppose you'll be taking the trail to the orchard and not the wagon?" That was too bad. She loved riding in the wagon, and it would be even better if she could sit beside someone as handsome as Brandon Bennett.

"Can't." He patted his bag again. "I might miss some photo ops."

"I can pretend to be a bear if it helps soften the blow of being in civilization," she offered.

His laugh was a deep chuckling sound. Wow. She had thought Edmund was the perfect Bennett brother, but this one was the stuff of romance book covers and stolen moments reading about dashing heroes when one was supposed to be shelving books.

"Ah, there's Will. I'll let you know if I need a bear." He started walking away, and she let him go for a few steps before following behind him.

He definitely looked as good from behind as he did from the front.

"Are you following me?" he asked with a glance over his shoulder.

"Yep."

"Why?"

"Because Lacey is why I am here." The only reason she was here. Because in all honesty, a church shindig was not where she belonged. That point had been made very clear to her a couple of years ago – the last time she had attended anything church-related.

He stopped walking. "Well, then, hurry up, and we can walk together." He waved her forward, and she scampered towards him.

"Thanks, but I really didn't mind the scenery from behind." She pressed her lips together. "I'm sorry. That was inappropriate." She had been trying to control her tongue ever since that day in the library when

Lacey had told her why she didn't like it when Trish said flirtatious things like that to Edmund.

He smiled at her. "I'm not."

Well, that was good to know, but she should still try to keep her admiration of him inside her mind. This was a church event, after all. Prim and proper were the words of the day if she did not want another set of churchgoers talking about her behind her back – or in her face with their fingers wagging out their condemnation of her.

"What brings you out of the woods?" Will teased his brother as they joined him and Lacey.

"You and your pretty half," Brandon returned as he gave Lacey a hug. "Mom wants pictures."

"Of us?" Lacey asked in surprise.

"Yep," Brandon answered.

"Oh." She kind of drew out the word and looked at Will. "How many?"

Brandon shook his head. "I don't know. Just however many I can get while we're here."

"Do we have to be together?" Lacey asked.

Brandon's brow furrowed. "That's the idea. Why?"

"I wasn't planning to spend the whole time with Will."

"You weren't?" Both Brandon and Trish said together.

"No. We're here together, but we are not inseparable."

Trish looked at Will to gauge his reaction to that comment. She knew how many times he came into the library in a week to see his fiancé. It wasn't daily, but it was close to it.

"Today's yours," Will said to Trish.

"What?" Trish looked from him to Lacey.

"I invited you," Lacey said. "It would be rather unthinking of me to invite you to come apple picking with me and then ignore you."

"But –?" Well, that was different. All her former friends had made her feel like an add-on as soon as they had a boyfriend or fiancé or husband.

"I guess I can take pictures of you and Trish, and maybe we can sneak a few of you and Will in there, too?" Brandon looked from Lacey to Trish. "Are you ok with that?"

"Me?" These were the most unusual people Trish had met. "Are you? Taking pictures is why you are here."

"I'll still be taking pictures," he assured her. "If you'll let me."

"Of course, I'll let you," she replied. "But I didn't know I was going to be doing more than taking selfies today."

"You look great," Lacey assured her as she linked

her arm through Trish's. "Come on, we have to go pay for our bags and get in line for the wagon."

"What's Will going to do?"

"He has four brothers and three of them are going to be here. Then, there's also Nate and Emma and Cari and –"

"Ok, I get it," Trish interrupted. "He won't be lacking for people to keep him company, but won't he still get lonely?"

"Absence makes the heart grow fonder."

"I'm not going that far," Will said from behind them. "It's a small group today. Only about twenty of us."

Twenty church people. Ok. She could do this. She knew at least a few of them – like Will, Lacey, Edmund, and Brandon – would accept her. Or so it seemed.

"I'm glad you came," Lacey whispered.

"Let me get the bags," Will offered when they reached the front of the entrance line. "We're all doing the corn maze, too, right?"

"Sure," Trish answered. "I heard this year's maze is pretty good, and there haven't been any storms through to knock it down yet."

"This year's is great. Hey, Trish. It is Trish, right?"

"Yep, that's me, and I'm going to say since you don't look almost exactly like Edmund that you're Henry."

He tapped his forehead. "That's putting the old grey matter to good use. Speaking of Eddie, has anyone seen him yet?"

"He went in with Cari, Nate, and Emma," Will answered.

"Good to see you, Brandon," Henry clapped him on the shoulder. "Keep the camera away from me."

"Don't worry. I wouldn't want to break it."

Henry laughed. "I just didn't want to outshine all the others." He struck a pose, held it for ten seconds, and then hit another.

"Wow," Trish muttered. "No lack of self-assurance there."

"Meh," Henry said, "a lot can be hidden behind a dose of swagger." His eyes challenged her to believe that he was only playing the role of an outgoing, devil-may-care guy.

"I suppose that's true," she agreed as she took the bag Will handed her. "I've known a person or two who hide in plain sight behind daring façades." She looked at one in the mirror every morning when getting ready to present herself to the world outside of her apartment.

Henry's eyes narrowed the tiniest bit, and he held her gaze for five loud heartbeats before nodding and saying, "I suppose we all know someone like that. Probably more than we realize we do."

Why did she feel like she had just been put through an x-ray machine and her soul had been laid bare? Henry was one Bennett brother to stay away from if she wished to keep her secrets to herself.

"Are you ready?" Lacey asked.

A camera clicked. "Ready," Brandon answered before stepping outside and drawing a deep breath.

He had been inside a building – a shack really – for maybe five minutes, and yet, he looked as if he had been missing the outdoors.

"It's a beautiful day," Lacey said.

He nodded. "I'm so glad I live in a world where there are Octobers."

"Have you read Anne of Green Gables?" Trish asked him.

He shook his head. "No, but I've seen the movies and read that quote on social media every day for the last week. It's mixed in with all the Thanksgiving and pumpkin spice stuff."

"You need to follow different people," Will said.

"Nah, I'd rather see that than some of the other stuff that gets posted. Besides," he said as they moved to the front of the line to get on the wagon, "I like Thanksgiving and pumpkin spice – especially pumpkin spice cookies – and I think it's good to have hallmarks of a season to look forward to. It makes one feel..." he looked off to the trees in the distance, "right."

Will offered his hand to Lacey. "May I help you ladies board the wagon?"

"Help Lacey," Trish said. "I can manage on my own. Thanks."

"Are you sure?"

"Perfectly." And then when she got on, she would try to find a place to sit other than where Will should be sitting – next to Lacey.

"After you," Brandon said to her, blocking Henry with his elbow.

"Can I sit with you?" she whispered to him. "I don't want to come between them." She tipped her head toward Will and Lacey. It was lovely that Lacey was not leaving Trish behind just because she was engaged, but Trish was not about to take advantage of it. If it were her, she'd want to snuggle up to her fiancé to ward off the nip of the mid-October wind.

"You could sit with me." Henry leaned around Brandon and fluttered his lashes.

That guy really did seem sure of himself. Another good reason to keep away from him.

"Sorry, but I prefer Brandon," she said.

"Ouch." He grasped his heart as if wounded.

"Please?" she said to Brandon.

"Of course. I should get some pictures of them on

the wagon anyway." He gave his brother a taunting look. It was not an unfamiliar thing for her to see Bennett brothers sparring with each other through looks and words. They all seemed to have pretty good relationships with each other, unlike her and some of her family.

"Thanks," she said to Brandon. "Will and Lacey are really great together, aren't they?" She watched her step as she approached the wooden steps to the wagon, being careful to avoid the evidence that they were not being pulled by a tractor but by horses.

"They really are," Brandon answered. There was a wistfulness to his tone that piqued her interest. "Maybe one day we'll all find that."

"Yeah, maybe," she agreed. Not that she believed it. Maybe it would happen for Brandon and Henry, but not her. Never for her.

~*~

Read Trish's story in Hatfield Falls (Don't Tell) book 2, *Don't Tell My Heart It Can Heal*, publishing in 2022. Sign up for Annilee's email list for updates on this series and discover if it is Brandon or Henry who is the next Bennett brother to find a happily ever after.

About the Author

Annilee Nelson writes faith-filled sweet romances from a cozy corner in the living room of her just-outside-of-Halfax-Nova-Scotia home. She is a life-long lover of stories with her favorite sorts being those that include families, groups of friends, and, of course, romance. Like Mrs. Bennett in the Hatfield Falls series, Annilee loves Jane Austen, though not enough to name her children after Miss Austen's characters.

You can learn more about Annilee, her books, and Nova Scotia (the setting for Hatfield Falls) by signing up for her newsletter at bit.ly/Annilee_NL. You can also find her on Facebook and Mewe and at annileenelson.com.